16

THE
WORLD
BENEATH

THE
WORLD
BENEATH

JANICE WARMAN

CANDLEWICK PRESS

Copyright © 2014 by Janice Warman

With thanks to Tony Brutus for kind permission to include "I am the exile," by Dennis Brutus © 1968 Dennis Brutus

First U.S. edition 2016

Library of Congress Catalog Card Number 2015931429
ISBN 978-0-7636-7856-2

16 17 18 19 20 21 BVG 10 9 8 7 6 5 4 3 2 1

Printed in Berryville, VA, U.S.A.

This book was typeset in Fairfield.

Candlewick Press
99 Dover Street
Somerville, Massachusetts 02144

visit us at www.candlewick.com

For Dominic and Imogen,
my first critics:

They are my best work,
Yet they are theirs alone,
Creating themselves anew, every day.

I am the exile

I am the exile,
am the wanderer
the troubadour
(whatever they say)

gentle I am, and calm
and with abstracted pace
absorbed in planning,
courteous to servility

but wailings fill the chambers of my heart
and in my head
behind my quiet eyes
I hear the cries and sirens

Dennis Brutus

PART ONE
1976

Chapter One

I f he stretched his fingers out in the dark, he could feel a damp wall. His head throbbed. How long had he been here? He lay quietly. There was an earth floor beneath him. His hands—he brushed the earth off them, then ran them over his face. It was sticky, and when he touched his nose, he cried out. One eye was swollen shut. On the back of his head, he found the source of his pain: a lump so big that it filled his hand.

It was quiet—a hollow kind of quiet that made him think he was alone in this place, wherever it was. He held his breath and listened. No birds sang. Yet this place must be in the veld. Perhaps it was a village. His stomach clenched in fear as he looked for a chink of light. Even at night a little light should leak in around a door; even in the country there was moonlight, starlight; even in the country there was movement, little rustles as things ran through the grass. Yet there was nothing. Perhaps he was dead. No, if he were dead, he would not feel pain. Or thirst. He was so thirsty. He felt around for a cup. Had someone left him some water?

He lay still again, with his dizzy head turned to one side, and resolved to think and to breathe slowly, to calm himself, to gather his strength so he could get out of here. He ran his hands over his body. He was dressed. He wriggled his toes. He had no shoes on, but his feet felt OK. Sometimes they went for your feet. Then, just as he thought, *I am going to roll over onto my hands and knees, crawl to the wall, and try to stand*—

The boy woke up. He was lying behind the comforting bulk of his mother. His heart was thudding fast. He shot out of bed and crouched against the far wall, arms over his head. "No!" he whispered before he could stop himself.

Then it came to him. The dream was about Sipho. In the dream, he *was* Sipho. His big brother, his strong, tall brother, who could swing him around and carry him high on his shoulders, Sipho with the deep laugh and wide, handsome face.

Before he'd thought what he was doing, he had shaken his mother awake. "Mama! Mama!" he sobbed. "Sipho! Sipho—he is hurt! I dreamed—I dreamed—"

His mother woke instantly. "No," she said gently. "No, he is working in Jo'burg and he sends us money. You know that. You mustn't worry." Slowly, he stopped crying and fell asleep again while she lay looking into the darkness, her arms around him, tears streaming down her face.

Presently, she saw threads of light between the door and its frame and slipped out of bed, disentangling her arms from the small body. Sipho used to sleep like that too, before he became a man. Before he went away to Jo'burg to earn a living. Before he sent money back to her in Cape Town and to her parents in the Ciskei, for her younger children. Before—

By this time she had crossed the yard and gone up the red stone steps to the back door. She slipped her key into the lock and raised a hand to her *doek,* tucking the scarf in neatly at the back. It was almost time to take up the tea.

Chapter Two

Beauty! Beauty! Where are you?" Mrs. Malherbe came rushing down the corridor and barged through the green baize door. "We need to sort out the menus before I can . . ."

Quickly, Joshua jumped into his hiding place by the kitchen. It was under the back stairs, which led out of the servants' hall, up to the first floor. It was a perfect space for him, and he sat here when he could, listening to the sounds of the house.

It was like a little room, a cupboard, really, into which the vacuum cleaner and the polisher were crammed. There wasn't much space left over, but there was enough for a boy with no shoes to crawl into the musty wooden dark. Joshua had pulled an old blanket in there once, one he had taken from Betsy's basket. She was a basset hound, who sometimes let him crawl in with her and give her a cuddle. There was a big fuss over the missing blanket. His mother had to swear that she hadn't taken it home or sold it.

"Sold it?" she fumed, as they sat in the damp paraffin smell of her room. "Why would I want to sell that old thing?" That was the trouble. They always thought you were stealing from them. Joshua didn't tell his mother he had the blanket, but she caught him anyway. She was getting the Hoover out of the cupboard when she found it.

"*Hayi,*" she said. "You have shamed me in front of the Madam. We must give it back." But he begged and pleaded, and in the end she left it where it was. At least that way, he supposed, she could say it had just somehow gotten into the cupboard; she didn't know how.

And it meant he was out of the way. In fact, he wasn't meant to be in the house at all. He should have been in the country with his grandparents. But Mrs. Malherbe was turning a blind eye, which was what these people did when they wanted to help you. Other times, they said, "How can I believe you?" or "You can't fool me—I'm not stupid."

They were, though. Most of them. How many of them could speak three or four languages? How many of them could run a house that size, cleaning it through every day, making the beds, doing the washing and the cooking, and still look after a set of fractious white children?

It seemed that most of them couldn't do anything at all. It took Mrs. Malherbe most of the morning to get up. Then she had coffee and buttered Provita by the pool and listened to *Woman's Hour.* After swimming ten lengths, she showered. Then she went out in her car. It was a dark green MG, and it made a throaty roar as it went up the road. Joshua loved that car. He washed it and polished it for her, twisting the cloth into little corners to get the last of the polish out of the little runnels under the windows

5

and buffing the chrome bumpers until they shone.

When he knew she was having a lie-down (something she did almost every afternoon), he sat in the tan leather driver's seat, running his hands over the cool steering wheel, gazing ahead down the driveway between the rows of smoke-blue hydrangeas, seeing the open road.

He was glad the Malherbes didn't have children, only a grown-up son who belonged to the Madam. He could hear the Websters across the road in the afternoons, and he shuddered. There were six of them: they screamed and fought and dive-bombed one another in the pool. Their mother shouted at them. But it was quiet by the time their father came home, and as dusk fell over the lawns, under the great gray back of the mountain, there was nothing to hear but the little hiss of sprinklers spitting and turning, spitting and turning.

Mr. Malherbe liked supper on the table at seven. There was, in consequence, a flurry of activity around six, when Mrs. Malherbe emerged pink-eyed from her bedroom and, clutching a gin and tonic, supervised the making of the supper and the setting of the table.

As far as Joshua could see, she did nothing but get in the way. She fussed and she tutted; she moved things; she tasted, screwing up her face; and as seven approached, and the second gin and tonic was poured, she retreated, combed her hair, put on a slash of red lipstick, and sat in the front lounge with the newspaper on her lap. At the sound of her husband's Mercedes, she held the paper up and looked earnestly at it. And there she would be when he came in.

The child was supposed to go to bed after supper in his mother's room, which was across the yellow dirt yard from the main house, between the garage, the workshop, and the outside bathroom. He would curl up in the sagging bed by the damp and peeling wall, head under the covers to keep out the light and the ceaseless sound of his mother's knitting machine. Often he would creep back to the big house across the yard, up the slippery red-polished steps of the back *stoep*, and curl up under the stairs, where it was warmer, and where now and then Betsy would crawl in with him.

He would hear them in the next room, having supper. Usually there was just a quiet rumble of talk; sometimes a shrill burst of laughter from Mrs. Malherbe. Sometimes he fell asleep, snug in his hairy cocoon, and woke to find Betsy snoring comfortably beside him. He would open the back door quietly, clicking the Yale lock shut behind him, and tiptoe out, the beaten yellow dust cold under his feet, and slip into bed behind his mother, staring into the darkness until sleep took him.

Often he would dream strange dreams that he knew were about Sipho: one night, a ring of mountains above his head, and he as small as an ant on the grass; in another, he was back in his grandparents' house in the Ciskei, hiding under the table with his little sister, Phumla, and giggling among the grown-ups' legs. Or he was all squashed up to one side in the back of a car; there was a cloth around his face, and he could only just breathe. His arms were tied behind him. He wriggled over onto his back and felt the fresh cold air come through the window onto his hot forehead, and in

7

the inky dark he saw stars, millions of stars. He was afraid. These were the dreams he hated the most, and they made him put off going to bed, even though his mother said Sipho was fine.

It was after supper one night, when he was in his hidey-hole under the stairs, that things changed. The tempo of the conversation quickened, and Mr. Malherbe's voice deepened. Mrs. Malherbe's voice ran quickly up the scale. He listened, holding his breath. She wasn't laughing. She was crying.

Then Mr. Malherbe roared, Mrs. Malherbe screamed, and something smashed. The front door slammed, and Joshua heard the iron gates crash open and the Mercedes's heavy tires squeal as it turned onto the road.

Chapter Three

Beauty picked up the broken bottle and dabbed at the wine stain on the wallpaper, her broad forehead a crosshatch of wrinkles. Mrs. Malherbe was a hard taskmistress; every day she would run her finger along the mantelpiece or a windowsill. "What's this, Beauty? What's this?" she would hiss. "I pay you to keep the house clean."

But she didn't do it today. She rang the bell for lemon tea and then emerged, hair in a turban, gown carelessly tied. She swam for an hour, up and down, with her head raised, paddling like an ungainly duck, and when Beauty asked her what to make for supper, she said, "Oh, Beauty, I don't know, you choose, I don't care, really—" She twisted the gown close around her and went dripping up the stairs. There was a faint yellow bruise at the base of her throat.

"Will the Master . . . ?" Beauty called after her, and trailed off. She turned and went silently, heavily, through the green baize door and into the kitchen.

The Master wouldn't; seven o'clock came and went, and at eight a yawning Beauty served the dried-out lamb chops, the wilting salad, wiped down the sink and the stovetop, and went.

The following evening, Mr. Malherbe's car turned in quietly through the gates and Mrs. Malherbe sat, mouth tight, looking carefully at the headlines and swirling her drink in the glass so that the ice cubes clinked.

Joshua quietly helped his mother in the kitchen, but he didn't go through with the plates. They both knew that Mr. Malherbe did not like him to be there, and all three of them ensured Joshua was not seen in the evenings.

Afterward, they both hurried across the backyard to the room. Beauty set her knitting machine going.

Finally he had to ask, "Mama, Mama, why am I here with you still?"

Beauty stopped the machine. She came and sat on the bed by him. She sighed. "Joshua, you were so sick." She took his hand and said, "We thought you were going to die." Tears brimmed at the edges of her eyes. "That's why I brought you to the city. I couldn't bear to leave you behind. What if . . . ?"

Joshua squeezed her hand. He remembered being ill, coughing and coughing, the fevers. He couldn't breathe; a few times he had coughed up browny-red stuff that he later realized was blood. He remembered waking in the night. His mother was always there, sitting by his bed; the gas lamp would be hissing, and she would be stitching.

He had been frightened. There would be a moment each time he woke when he would feel that cramp of terror in his stomach; then he would see she was there, and he would feel a little calmer.

There was one visit to the doctor, a thin, pale man behind a desk, who had shaken his head over the red-stained cloth they had shown him. Then Joshua had to sit up on the high bed on a crackling white paper sheet and the man said, "I'm sorry, Joshua, this is going to be cold. It's a stethoscope. I need to put it on your chest so I can listen to your breathing." It tickled a bit and he giggled, then had a fit of coughing that ended with more blood in the bowl.

They went into another room and he had to stand very still with a cold, flat plate against his chest, and the nurse left the room (but his mother didn't). Then there was a buzzing noise, and the nurse came back and slid out the big metal plate and put another one in. She told him to turn around and to stand very still again. Afterward, the doctor put the pictures up on a lighted panel; the light shone through the dark patches on the film.

"He'll need tablets." He wrote something on a piece of paper and handed it to Beauty. "It's very important that he has them three times a day with food." He turned to Joshua. "And you must finish all of them. Do you understand? We are lucky these days. Tuberculosis is curable. But you must take the tablets for a year."

He was still weak and feverish, and the tablets gave him the runs, but after a little while he began to feel better. They put a chair for him outside the hut, and there he sat in the sunshine, with his head back and his eyes closed.

At night Joshua lay in the dark of the back room on his own, because his mother did not want his sister and brother to catch his disease. It was carried on the air, she said; he was not to touch them and not to cough if he was near them.

But then it was time for his mother to go back to the city. She had had a letter from Mrs. Malherbe: "Beauty, I have been very patient. But now I need you to come back. If you are not back by next week, I will have to look for another maid." Then the arguments began.

His grandmother said, "Leave the boy with us."

His mother said, "No. No, I cannot . . . No, he is coming with me."

There was the big boom of his grandfather's voice, and his mother began to cry.

"Your Madam will sack you!" shouted his grandfather, and then there was the softer sound of his grandmother's voice, and his mother's, high and keening. "Then what will we all do?" he roared.

When the day came, it turned out that Joshua *was* to go with her to the city. It was the Easter holidays, and he was to be sent back to his grandparents when school started again.

Joshua didn't want to leave his sister, Phumla, and Xola, his younger brother. Phumla was small and thin, with little tight braids and big anxious eyes; she was his favorite. Xola was her twin, but he was sturdier and stronger; Joshua didn't worry about him so much. When his mother was away, he looked after them. He had to get them ready for school and make sure they ate their breakfast.

They climbed up into the truck. Joshua didn't know who was crying more, he or the twins. They clung to each

12

other, sobbing. He leaned out the window. His grandmother stood behind them with her hands on their small shoulders. His grandfather stood to one side, looking away, still angry.

But he had to be strong. He was their big brother. "Bye-bye!" he called down to them, waving. They looked so small. "Be good! I'll see you soon!"

He leaned over and waved again. "I'll bring you back a present!" he called.

Then they were off, bumping up the dusty track; he looked back and watched them getting smaller and smaller, waving. His grandfather, too, finally raised a hand, just before they turned the corner, and he couldn't see them anymore.

"So why am I still here?" Joshua asked his mother again. "The holidays are over."

Beauty hesitated. "I think it is better to keep you with me. It is safer."

"Why?"

"Because — because . . . I do not want to send you back on your own. It is not safe to send a boy a long way like that all alone."

"But *why*?"

She hesitated again. "Because Y's a crooked letter and you can't make it straight," she said finally, and a smile transformed her round, anxious face. "Go to sleep now."

Soon she was back at the knitting machine, and Joshua lay waiting to fall asleep to its comforting clatter, the smell of the damp plaster sharp in his nostrils.

* * *

He thought of his grandmother. When he came out with his blanket around him to sit in the sun at the front of their house, she would always open her arms to him and enfold him in a big strong hug.

"But, Grandmother," he would say, "you are not supposed to hug me. I will make you sick!"

And she would just laugh and hug him again and kiss the top of his head. "Nonsense," she would say. "I am so old I cannot get sick any longer. There is no sickness that I am afraid of now."

She was a big woman, broad and strong. His mother had her high cheekbones and wide mouth. She was not afraid of anything, least of all his grandfather, though his grandfather was tremendously tall and thin and leaned forward wherever he walked, as if he wanted to get where he was going as fast as he could. He had a terribly loud voice and a quick temper, and if Joshua hadn't grown up with them both and seen that his mother and his grandmother were not afraid of him, he would have found him terrifying.

As it was, Joshua thought that if he was not to have a father, then to have a grandfather like that was a good thing. A grandfather like that could protect you.

Today, though, he was still feeling weak. He was taking the tablets, but they had not yet begun to make him strong. He sat and leaned against his grandmother, the blanket around him, and closed his eyes, gratefully soaking in the rays of the sun.

Then she told him a story. He loved to tell stories to the twins, and he thought he must have gotten it from his grandmother. She could hold them all spellbound and silent; even when the twins were very small, they would hold on to each other's hands and look up at her with big eyes while she spoke.

"Joshua, have I told you the story about the great prophetess?" she asked.

"No, Grandmother."

"Then I will. One day," she began, "a young girl and her friend went to fetch water at the river. She had a vision. She saw her ancestors. They told her that the people must kill their cattle and a new age would come when the white people would be driven into the sea and they would have their land back again.

"Only it was wrong. It was all wrong." And his grandmother shivered. "The day came when the sun was supposed to rise up red like blood in the east and go down again in the east, and the white people were meant to run into the sea." She paused. "Only the sun came up as normal and went down as normal. No one was driven into the sea. And the people starved. Because no new cattle sprang up out of the furrows of the fields, as the prophecy had promised.

"Our people have never recovered from this. We are still under the foot of the foreigner. That is why we struggle, my child. And one day"—and she turned his face to hers and gave him a long, long look that made him shiver—"one day, perhaps you will be one of those who can help us to escape our prison. But that is a story for tomorrow. Now you are tired."

And it was true. Joshua felt so tired, he could hardly keep his eyes open.

When he went back inside, he fell straight into a deep sleep, and he saw piles of dead cattle and rows and rows of starving people, all on their knees, with their hands outstretched.

"Feed us, feed us!" they were crying. "Help us, or we will die." Some of them were little children.

He woke sobbing in the night, and then his mother was there.

He heard her speaking to his grandmother the next morning. "Why did you tell him that terrible story? He had a nightmare."

Then his grandmother's voice. It was harsh. "Sooner or later, he must know the truth. Living here, he is protected. But when he grows up, he will have to face it."

The next day, Sipho came. He hardly ever saw Sipho, but he came on the bus from Jo'burg because Joshua was ill. He looked gray with exhaustion.

They sat on the bench outside the house, talking in the late afternoon sun, Sipho's head tilted back against the wall, his eyes closed, his arm around Joshua.

"You look tired, my brother," said the boy. "Do they not treat you well?"

Sipho sighed. "It is not the work," he replied. "The work is hard, but I do not mind it." He paused. "You know that the government is unfair to us?" he asked, but it was not really a question. "You know how we are only allowed to work in certain jobs? And that our mother is not allowed to take you and the twins to live with her in Cape Town?"

"But I'm going!" said Joshua.

"Yes, you're going. But you are a special case. And besides,"—Sipho was talking more quickly now, almost as if he were talking to himself—"besides, these are only some of the things that are wrong with this country. We do not have any say"—he thumped the arm of his chair with every syllable as he spoke—"any say, any say at all." His big palm, rough with working, thumped the wooden arm of the big chair. "Any say in what happens to us: where we live, what work we do, how much we can earn."

He whipped around and took Joshua's chin in his hand, gazing into his eyes with a fervor Joshua had never seen before. "Joshua, you are too young, but when you grow up, you will see this country for what it is: a country in which we work like dogs but where we do not have any power!"

He leaned back and looked far into the distance. "Some of us are fighting the government. It is dangerous work. It is secret. And if they find out—" He broke off, as if he had only just remembered that he was speaking to his little brother.

Joshua lay very still and remembered that moment: Sipho's sideways glance and the way he had suddenly fallen silent. He remembered how he had felt shaky inside, like a great big dark cave had opened up in front of him and something was pushing him into it.

They hadn't spoken further, because his mother had

come and said it was time for Sipho to go back to Jo'burg. He and his mother walked with Sipho to the bus stop and waited. He felt suddenly afraid and squeezed Sipho's hand. Sipho laughed at him as he usually did, swung him around, teased him, and put his strong arms around their mother and hugged her hard as tears ran down her cheeks; they always did when Sipho went. But there was something in his eyes, something behind the big smile and the jokes, that made Joshua shiver. Soon after that, the dreams began.

Chapter Four

B oy . . ." said Mrs. Malherbe, pink-eyed at the side of the pool, her wet hair crimped close to her head. "Boy, tell your mother to get me some tea. And tell her to cut the lemon thin."

He ducked his head and ran. His job during the day was to keep out of the way but to be within earshot. Then Mrs. Malherbe didn't have to shout for Beauty.

She had been quieter in the last few days. Mr. Malherbe came and went as before, but after supper he went straight into his study and shut the door. Mrs. Malherbe put records on the big walnut stereo in the front lounge. From the speakers, a man's voice sang "Dream a Little Dream of Me."

Joshua took to creeping into the house again after supper. The Cape autumn was crisping the oak leaves at their edges, and it was colder in the evenings. But the house was always warm, the kitchen especially.

He was pulling Betsy's long ears and talking quietly to her when he heard the noises from the dining room. A thump and then a gasp. He held his breath and expelled it slowly. Silence. Then another thump. But no talking, no shouting.

Then another gasp, a silence, and the beginning of a thin wail, like a young baby's cry, weak and powerless: "Oh, Gordon . . ." Then nothing.

Terrified, he scrambled out of the cupboard and made for the back door, but he wasn't fast enough. The dining-room door was flung open so violently it crashed against the wall. Mr. Malherbe brushed past his crouched form, unseeing. He grabbed his keys from the rack and was gone.

Trembling, Joshua hesitated on the threshold of the dark yard. His mother's light was out. He turned back into the house. Mrs. Malherbe was not in the study or the lounge or the dining room. He listened at the foot of the stairs. He could hear the bath running.

In the morning, Mrs. Malherbe lay as if dead by the swimming pool, her hips jutting at the edges of her yellow swimsuit. There was a purple stain on her arm. Her mouth looked odd; it was turned down at one side. A little closer, he could see that the whole side of her face was puffy and yellow. Sunglasses hid her eyes.

"Boy!"

She glared at him, her iron-colored hair twisted into waves close to her head. "I want you to get me some cigarettes. Can you do that? Twenty Viceroys. There's money on the hall table."

"Yes, Madam."

"And, boy?"

"Yes, Madam?"

"Don't stare—it's rude."

Joshua opened the gate and looked up and down the street. It was quiet in the midday sun, pools of shade under the big oaks spilling out into a desert of melting tarmac. The one-rand note was damp in his hand. He pushed it down into his pocket and set off.

It was only a quarter of a mile to the shop, but Joshua hated the journey. He hesitated at the edge of the shade and made a dash, gasping at the heat beneath his bare feet. He hopped from foot to foot, then continued, skirting the big iron gates where the Dobermans lurked.

They always flew at him with such ferocity that he was sure the latch would give and they would burst through. He would be sure they were locked away in the back courtyard, and then just as he passed they would rush out after him, mouths wide with longing.

Today they didn't, though, and he was just making his usual hop, skip, and jump down one side of the street, thinking he was in the clear—there were no more gates, the shop was only around the corner now—when a police van turned onto the street.

His mind went blank. This was the very worst thing that could happen. Here he was, on a white street, with money in his pocket. His mother had told him, "My boy, you must never let the police see you. You are not supposed to be here. You must be invisible. Our people are not allowed in white areas unless we have a pass to work here."

But to his astonishment, the big Black Maria eased on

21

by, then picked up speed as the siren gave voice and the orange light began to spin.

He ran straight across the intersection, along the burning pavement, around the corner, and into the half-light of Mr. Koegel's shop.

"TwentyViceroyplease," he said quickly, before seeing that Mrs. Ellis was standing by the counter. Mrs. Ellis lived across the road from the Malherbes and because of her age, her mountainous size, and her heart condition was rarely seen this far from home.

"*Tsssk*," she tutted at him. Then she winked without smiling. "Serve him first," she said briskly to Mr. Koegel. "I want a good gossip. And we don't want to keep Mrs. Malherbe waiting for her cigarettes, do we, boy?"

On the way back, Joshua took the short route, running under the tunnel of trees on Elsie's Road. As he passed under the last one, there was a loud crack and he looked up. A face, ashen with fright, gazed out halfway up the tree; a pair of legs pedaled the air.

"Help me, man!" a voice said. It happened so fast. Almost without thinking, Joshua reached up and quickly gave the man a leg up, higher into the branches. The man gave an "oof!" of pain. Joshua's heart began a *rat-tat-tat* he could almost hear.

He was still gazing up when a voice barked in his ear. "*Wat doen jy?* What are you doing?" It was the policeman again, in the van with the cage on the back. Dumbly, shaking, he held up Mrs. Malherbe's cigarettes and gestured down the road.

"*Weg is jy!*" said the driver. "Go! Away with you!" He rolled his eyes and made an upward shrug of exasperation. The van rolled on down the road, but slowly, the two men inside glancing through the gateways and into the hedges.

There was a faint rustle. "Hey, thanks, man," said the voice. Joshua dropped to one knee and made as if to tie a shoelace on his bare foot. He looked covertly up the road. The Black Maria was gone.

He looked up into the tree. "That's OK. Just don't do that too many times. Next time I'll have a heart attack."

The dark face looking out at him was laughing, the teeth even and white, eyes brown and merry. But the left eye was half closed and the lip was cut.

"Hey, where you staying, then? I'll come see you."

"Number twenty-three."

And Joshua, released from the thrall of that smile, ran.

Mrs. Malherbe had retired to rest. His mother shook her head and raised her eyes to heaven. The Madam was not happy. He was in trouble. He had taken too long.

He went down to the pool, still thinking about the man. Who was he? Why were the police looking for him? There were frogs in the filter basket. He went to fish them out, hoping they would still be alive. But they were floating, pale bellies up, turning slowly, legs trailing, little hands in the gesture of surrender.

Then, as he reached among the cold bodies for the handle, he saw it, clinging to a broken tile, its little emerald body quaking, breaths pulsing its sides in and out.

He lifted the young frog out on his fingers, cupping it

23

in both hands. He decided to keep it. Turning this problem over in his mind, he went down the garden toward the compost heap.

He would need to stop it from getting back to the pool. But how? And what could he feed it? He didn't even know what it ate. And what if he made a little home for it and then Goodman the gardener came, and—

A hand closed over his wrist. He dropped the frog. *"Aaai-eee!"* He looked up.

"Hello."

The man smiled at him. Joshua could see that his lip had begun to bleed. "Hey, you saved my life, man. I owe you." He dabbed his mouth with the back of his hand.

Joshua found his voice. "So what did you do? Why were the police looking for you?"

The smile shut off like a switch. "One day I'll tell you."

"Hey, come!" Joshua pulled at him. "They mustn't see you. Go to the old shed. Down the path behind the plane trees and through the hedge. I'll get you some tea."

The man resisted for a moment. Then he switched on the smile again and went. He was dragging his left leg, Joshua could see, and wincing with each step.

Chapter Five

Joshua ran up to the house, down the winding path, through the gap in the hedge, and concealed himself behind the high wall that bordered the yard. He peeked through the gate. The coast was clear; the cars were gone from the garage. It was safe to go in.

He hesitated on the threshold of the door into the back hall, one foot still on the red-polished *stoep*. Betsy raised her long head from the basket and regarded him mournfully. He raised his finger to his lips. She laid her head on her extended paws, ears folding like puddles of brown velvet over her short legs and onto the blanket.

He tore into the kitchen and skidded about on the cold tiled floor, gathering what he needed. He could hear the Hoover upstairs. His mother was in the hallway; that meant she had finished with all six bedrooms and would be down soon.

Two ragged hand-cut slices of brown bread—no time to use the tabletop slicer; between them he pressed thick pieces of ham and a smear of mustard. To this he added a tomato, a chunk of cucumber, a spill of salt. An apple. He used a tin plate, one of those kept solely for use by Goodman and his mother. By then the kettle had boiled, and he filled a tin mug with hot water, milk, a tea bag, a spoon, and three spoons of sugar. Then he was back on the path, gingerly balancing plate and cup.

The man had found the shed, half hidden behind the stand of poplars at the far end of the garden. He was sitting on the ground with his back against the door, which was overgrown with Virginia creeper. He said nothing, just took the food. He ate it fast, downing the tea in three big gulps, and only when he had the apple in his hand and had taken a big bite out of it did he stop and say, "Hey, thanks. What's your name?"

"Joshua," said Joshua. Greatly daring, he asked again, "What did you do? Why were the police—"

The man gave him an earnest look and laid a big hand over his small one. "Honest to God, Joshua, it's better if you don't know."

"Please," said Joshua. "I'd like to help you."

"You already saved me." And the man gave him a grin that didn't quite reach his eyes. He looked wary. "Look, Joshua, I need a place to stay for a few days." He gestured at his left leg, which the boy could now see was extremely swollen, stretching the ragged trouser leg.

For the first time, Joshua felt afraid.

"My name is Tsumalo," the man said. "Tell me about this place."

Joshua said slowly, "There is a Madam and a Master. There are no children. Then there is Mama, and Goodman the gardener. He only comes here two days.

"Mama is the maid," he added. He fell silent for a moment, then continued. "This shed isn't used. No one comes down here. There is a new shed for the lawn mower, and Goodman uses that when he comes."

The man was quiet. He regarded Joshua closely, as if he was weighing up whether to trust him. Joshua could see that his arms, mostly bare under a torn and faded green shirt, were bruised and swollen. His feet were bare, and his trousers, which had once been khaki, were stained and torn at the hem.

"I've been on the run," he said slowly. "They"—he said this with a jerk of the head—"are after me. I did something—something they didn't like."

"What?" asked Joshua, emboldened by the man's sudden eloquence.

But Tsumalo hesitated. "Joshua, it's safer if you don't know. If they catch up with me, then they will arrest everyone who could have seen me, and that could include you. What you don't know, you can't tell." He stopped again. "Do you know what we are fighting for?"

"No-o-o-o-o," said Joshua slowly, reluctant to admit it. He thought of what Sipho had told him. "Well, a little bit—"

"We are fighting for freedom, Joshua. The whites have the power, and they don't want to share it with us. They call it *apartheid*."

He stopped and regarded Joshua again. "Do you know what a democracy is, Joshua?"

"No." Again he was embarrassed. It was a word he had never heard before.

"In the olden days, people were ruled over by kings and queens, or by the leader of a tribe. Nowadays, in most of the world, people have a say in who rules over them. They can choose who they like. They can vote. And each person gets one vote."

This sounded exciting to Joshua. He had heard of kingdoms when his mother read to him about Robin Hood, who robbed the rich to give to the poor, and about the evil King John and the brother he had exiled, Richard the Lionheart. But then Richard was also a king, and he was good . . .

"But here," continued Tsumalo, "here only the whites have votes."

"But that's not fair!"

"No. No, that's not fair, Joshua, and we are fighting to change it. We want one man, one vote." And he paused. "And one woman too, of course."

For a brief and wonderful moment, Joshua imagined his mother living in the big house, waking up in the bay-windowed master bedroom with its gray silk bedspread and its fancy cream-and-gold-painted dressing table with the curly legs and the triple mirror. But just as he got to the part where he had to think who would bring her tea in, her strong Five Roses tea with the sweet Carnation milk—

"Hey," said Tsumalo. "Your mother will want to know where you are."

Joshua smiled at him. "I will bring you blankets and food tonight. Don't worry. I will look after you." And he ran off down the path, heart thudding with excitement.

But when Joshua got back to the house, there was trouble. "Where have you been?" shouted his mother, grabbing him by the arm. It hurt. Her face was all twisted up as if she was in pain. He had never seen her look like this.

"Mama, Mama," he said, "don't worry, I'm fine, I was just . . . I was just"—and he was going to say that he was clearing the filter basket, but she saw his hesitation and pounced on it.

"Where were you? Where?"

She hadn't been able to find him. There had been talk of the police wagon cruising the streets looking for a fugitive.

"I thought—" she said.

She hadn't known what to think.

So he told her. He told her that the man whom the police were hunting was in their garden, in the old broken-down hut behind the poplar trees. That he was injured. That Joshua had taken food to him.

"No!" she cried, crushing her fist to her mouth. "He cannot stay! It will end badly for us. For all of us."

She crossed to the sink, washed her hands, and dried them. She peered into the kettle's shiny surface and wiped her eyes. She straightened her *doek*. And when she was ready, she took his hand and said, "Take me to him."

Down the garden path they went, past Goodman's shed, which was painted green and had a camp chair outside by the neat row of outdoor brooms and rakes, each suspended on their hooks. Through the gap in the hedge, on down to the overgrown part of the yard where the compost heap was, and where the path was overarched by a tangle of wild,

29

dusky pink bougainvillea, and to the row of poplars, and behind them, to the old shed.

As they approached, Tsumalo emerged, his head festooned with cobwebs that he was attempting to brush out of his eyes. He froze as he saw them.

"What are you *doing?*" Joshua had never heard his mother speak like that to anyone. She seemed different this afternoon.

The smile vanished. He put his hands out in a placatory gesture. "I do not mean to bring you trouble. The boy said —"

"The *boy?*" Beauty sounded scornful. "You mean to say that you are taking your instructions from a boy?"

Joshua was shocked. He drew away from his mother.

Tsumalo did not look at him. He said again, "I do not mean to bring you trouble. But I would beg you —"

"Do not *beg* me," she cut in.

Tsumalo said again, "I beg you for shelter. I promise you I won't stay long. If they find me, I will swear no one knew I was here."

"And they will believe you?" But Beauty's tone had softened imperceptibly, and Joshua knew that by now she had overlooked his height and his commanding presence and seen, as he had, the bruises, the injuries, the swollen leg, the ragged clothing, the bare feet.

Both of them paused for a moment, looking at each other, and into Joshua's mind came irresistibly the sentences from the Bible that he had heard in Sunday school, back home: *"For I hungered, and ye gave Me meat; I was thirsty, and ye gave Me drink; I was a stranger, and ye took Me in . . ."*

And as if she herself had heard these words, Joshua's mother dropped her gaze to the ground at her feet.

"You can stay. But you are not to leave the shed; the boy will bring you food."

She crossed the few paces between them, took Tsumalo's left hand in hers, and ran practiced fingers gently over the swellings, grazes, and bruises on his arms; her fingers hovered near the cuts on his lip and beside his swollen eye.

"Joshua, run quick now and get a basin with hot water and some towels, and the Dettol." She did not look at him. "Make sure the Madam doesn't see you."

Chapter Six

It was unbearably hot, and the top of the stable door was open to the night. Every now and then, a brown shiny rose beetle flew into the room at great speed, buzzing and banging against the walls and the bare lightbulb that hung from the ceiling before whizzing out again into the dark.

Across the dirt yard, a light was on in the kitchen; Mrs. Malherbe was making herself a cup of tea. In the corner of the big room, he knew, was a pantry, with shelves packed to the ceiling with biscuits and tea and rusks and flour and sugar and jam and preserves; there were also a fat-bellied fridge and a huge chest freezer, into which the Madam would lean on Saturdays to pull out a lamb roast to defrost for Sunday.

There was a big fireplace, though there was never a fire in it—fires were reserved for the living room—and there was plenty of room to slide around the polished red-tiled floor in his socks, if the Malherbes were out.

"Mama, why is Tsumalo in trouble?" Joshua was sitting

on the bed with his exercise book balanced on his knee, frowning at the letters he was carefully forming.

Beauty looked up and stopped the knitting machine for a moment. "It is very difficult to explain," she said.

She didn't want to, he could see.

"Why did they hurt him like that?" he asked.

It had upset him to see how Tsumalo had winced silently as his mother had sponged the wounds and dressed them with the scarlet Mercurochrome, which was all he could find in the downstairs bathroom cabinet, and which somehow made them look much worse.

She had made him take his shirt off, and they had both gasped at what it revealed: a burn mark the size of a hand, blistered and suppurating, on his back.

His mother's face had set like stone, and her mouth had gone into the hard straight line that told him she was angry.

"I will need a proper dressing for this," she had said quietly.

The back of Beauty's hand had once looked like that, when the iron had slipped out of her grasp. She had screamed, and Mrs. Malherbe had run in from the living room and taken her straight to the hospital.

Joshua ran for the big first-aid kit under the kitchen sink. When he got back, gasping for breath, he could see that his mother had been crying. Her eyes were red. She and Tsumalo were speaking quietly, but stopped when they saw him.

When she had finished dressing the wound, she stood and gently fed the shirt back over his head as he sat on the camp stool and put his arms through the sleeves as if he were a child. "Now the leg," she said. Quickly she knelt and cut the ragged trouser leg. Joshua saw that Tsumalo's leg was swollen and bruised from thigh to calf. Beauty frowned at it and looked up at the man sitting awkwardly on the camp stool. "Do you think it is broken?"

"I had to jump," he said. "It was a long way down. I fell when I landed. I can put my weight on it, but it hurts."

"Then you cannot go from here. You will have to rest your leg until it is better."

She stood slowly and looked down at him.

"I will send the boy with food and clothing," she said formally.

"Thank you, sister. *Hamba kahle*. Go well," he said.

Joshua half raised his hand in a salute and turned to follow his mother. He didn't feel like speaking. He could sense her anger, but he knew it was not for him. He wanted to catch her up and hold her hand, but he somehow knew she would shake it off.

At suppertime he took Tsumalo a plate of *tamatie-bredie*, lamb stewed with tomatoes, on a big pile of mashed potatoes and spinach; an old walking stick he found under the stairs; and, over his arm, neatly ironed and darned, some trousers and a shirt of Mr. Malherbe's that had been put aside to be thrown out. His mother had always taken these clothes, made them good, and put them to one side for any of her relatives who might need them.

"Waste not, want not," she said as she packed them

away, something Mrs. Malherbe always declared whenever she decided they would have leftovers for supper.

As he went back along the path, he considered how he could keep the shed hidden. He would make the path look unused by pulling fallen branches across it; he would pull down strands of the bougainvillea. But as he got to the gap in the hedge, he had a better idea: behind the new shed, he found an old wheelbarrow with a broken wheel and tipped it up, as if it had just been propped against the hedge to get it out of the way.

He stepped back and looked. Now there was no gap. Or you couldn't see it, anyway.

He went on his way, pleased with himself. Of course Goodman would notice; but Joshua would explain it to him. Joshua knew he would be happy to help a brother.

He remembered the baby frog and went to look for it. It was back in the filter basket, clinging to the side, its little chest pumping with the effort of breathing through the chemical fumes. He picked it out gently and found a big cardboard box. He could make a little pool out of a bowl and put leaves in it.

The little frog shook in his hands, terrified. Joshua paused for a moment. It might not be good for it to be kept in a box. He decided to keep it in there until he could take it across to the common and release it into the pond.

The trouble was that the frogs thought the swimming pool was a beautiful blue pond. But once they jumped into it, they found it was toxic and couldn't get out. Then the filter system drew them in, and they ended up in the filter basket, dead or dying.

He thought of Tsumalo, who had escaped, and wondered how long he would stay, and whether the police would come and find him.

Not if he could help it.

Chapter Seven

Mama . . ." Joshua was sitting at the kitchen table, kicking the metal legs, drinking milk out of a tin mug. A question was forming in his brain, but he hadn't quite decided what it was when she gave him a sharp kick on the shin, whisked the mug out of his hands, and leaped to her feet.

Mr. Malherbe walked in. Joshua kept his eyes fixed on the floor. He was breathing fast. Had he conjured him up? He'd been thinking about him, had been about to ask his mother . . . and he wasn't supposed to be in here . . .

He felt himself being raised off his seat like a puppy, by the scruff of the neck, his shirt bunched and choking. Mr. Malherbe's breath was hot on his ear.

"*What* is this boy doing in here? Drinking our milk? Eating our food? What have I told you, Beauty?"

"I'm sorry, Master. I'm sorry." Her voice was light with fright.

The man moved to the door, his grip tightening, and with one swift movement he threw Joshua into the yard, as you might throw a cat or a bowl of water.

Joshua landed silently, heavily, a choking in his throat as his knees and elbows skinned in the yellow grit.

"I don't want to see him in here again — understand? Otherwise he goes. And that's it."

The kitchen door slammed. The baize door swung and swung on its heavy hinges. Joshua scrambled to his mother's room and jumped into the bed, pulling the covers over his head.

In the kitchen, Beauty silently washed the dishes.

Upstairs, in the house, another door banged.

Presently, Joshua ran to find Tsumalo, who held him at arm's length, looked grimly down at the grazed knees, then hugged him. They walked slowly to the far end of the yard, where the pool lay quietly limpid behind its high hedges, Tsumalo leaning on the walking stick. They sat on the steps, and he washed Joshua's knees and elbows off with the water. It stung. The blood floated away in spiral whispers. Joshua watched, distracted; he wanted to make more of them. They went too quickly.

Tsumalo made him some hot sweet tea over the paraffin stove in the shed and watched him drink it. Only then did he speak.

"You want me to fix him?"

"Who?"

"Him." A sullen jerk of the head toward the house, a sneer at the corner of the mouth. "Mr. High-and-Mighty."

"*No!*" Joshua almost shouted. "No — you can't."

"Can't I? That's what they like to think. That we can't. Do. Anything." Tsumalo's face was rigid with anger.

38

Joshua was silent. He looked down. This was not his Tsumalo. This was somebody else. Somebody who frightened him.

Just as Joshua moved to go back to his mother, Tsumalo put his hand out in a conciliatory gesture. "Don't worry," he said more gently. "I won't." He paused. "It's not time. Not yet."

Chapter Eight

After that, Joshua kept to his mother's room until he was sure Mr. Malherbe had gone each morning. He kept out of his way when he came home, late and angry after an evening at the club, hefting his dried-up supper out of the warming oven and straight into the trash.

Then he would take a last brandy out to the chair by the pool. Joshua, sitting in the fig tree, had learned the art of silence and sat still as a leaf. Just once a fig fell, dislodged by his slipping foot, and crushed its split redness on the man's shoulder.

He cursed and flicked it away, and Joshua held his breath until the tall, stooped figure rose and stumbled into the house.

Each afternoon Joshua was anxious that Mr. Malherbe would come back early from work, pop home for lunch, or swing by to pick up his clubs and take an afternoon off to play golf. He had never, to his knowledge, done any of these things. But Joshua devised a plan, just in case: he found he could climb the loquat tree in the front garden and stay completely hidden in its glossy dark leaves. He had a good view of the front gate and the section of road up which the silver Mercedes purred each evening, never early; often late.

In any case, every evening he could hear the car approaching, at which sound he dropped to the loamy ground and hurtled along the narrow alley at the side of the house, tripping over the tangle of nasturtiums in his haste to reach his mother's room.

He was in the tree now, watching the sun make the gray pavement sparkle, blurring his eyes and bringing them back into focus, over and over again, until they ached.

There was a noise from the next-door garden. He looked down. A little girl was pushing a toy lawn mower back and forth, back and forth, humming to herself. *"Vrrrm, vrrrm. Vrrrm, vrrrm."* She was wearing a flouncy yellow dress of the kind favored by white Madams for their daughters, until their daughters got old enough to hate them.

Joshua had a sudden desire to frighten her. She looked so cute and smug. So plump and well-fed. Phumla, who lived so far away with his grandparents, had never had a dress like that.

Before he knew he had done it, he had flung a loquat at the girl. But his aim was faulty and it landed short. She stopped pushing the lawn mower and picked up the hard yellow fruit. Then she looked at the tree. Joshua sat perfectly still.

She walked over to the corner of the lawn and looked up.

She couldn't see him. Could she? She could. She smiled a fat little smile at him, a confident smile.

41

"Hello. What are you doing up there? Are you the boy Hester says is living next door? Should we have a loquat feast? I love loquats, but Mummy says I mustn't have them. She says they give me a runny tummy!" And she laughed.

She started climbing up the wooden fence.

"No!" he said. "You mustn't. Stay down there—I'll throw some down." Anything to stop her. He could see it—her mother would glance out at the lawn and find her precious angel gone. She would find she was up a tree with the black boy from next door. And he would be in trouble. Big trouble.

He began to tear the loquats off the branches, desperately, and toss them down. Then he stopped. Half of them were unripe. She would get the runs. And she would tell her mother how she'd gotten them.

Joshua stalled. "They'll make you sick. They're green. Wait here—I'll get you something better." He jumped to the ground and gathered some nasturtiums, the yellow and orange flowers thick in his hands, their sticky green stems trailing, and climbed back up.

He reached down over the fence and gave them to her. "Try these—you can suck the nectar out. They're sweet."

She looked skeptical. But she tried one, grimacing, and then her round face lit up under the heavy brown bangs. "They're like fairy sweets!" She grasped them tight. "Get me some more."

It wasn't a request.

He climbed down again, and as he did he heard Hester's voice. "Miss Anna, you must come in for your bath now."

"O-o-o-o-o-oh," said Anna. "But I'm busy, Hester!"

He could hear a rising whine in her voice.

"Come along now, Miss Anna." Hester's voice was weary.

It reminded him. He had heard Hester tell his mother: "Madam is kind, but that Miss Anna—she is like the boss of the house! Even the Master worries what Anna wants."

His mother had said: "It's because she was sick when she was little." She nodded toward Joshua and dropped her voice. "And Mrs. Brown, she . . ." and he missed the rest. "So they can't have any more . . ."

Any more what? He never found out.

Chapter Nine

It seemed that Miss Anna had decided she liked him. The next day, when he climbed the tree, she was waiting for him in the next-door garden.

"Boy!" she called imperiously. "Boy! Come down! I want to play with you!"

Not if he could help it. He slithered down the trunk as quietly as he could and tiptoed along the alley by the high wooden fence that separated the yards, but she was ahead of him. Just as he emerged into the dusty backyard, he heard a breathless giggle and saw her wide blue eye at a knothole in the fence.

Later he appealed to his mother. She shook her head and sighed. There was nothing you could do about the vagaries of white people. Even their children. He would have to live with it. Stay away from the fence. Keep his head down. Stay out of trouble.

He went down the overgrown path to find Tsumalo and gave the whistle that they used as a code. Tsumalo opened the door a crack and beckoned him in. He listened to Joshua's story, then smiled and put his warm hand on Joshua's head.

"You are already having trouble with the women. It is because you are so handsome. It is your own fault."

And he said no more, just laughed and picked up his notebook as if to say, *I have more important things to worry about. Grown-up things.*

The next day Anna came visiting. He heard the gate clang and the footsteps on the path and the confident knock on the front door. Beauty answered; it was after lunch, and Mrs. Malherbe had gone straight up to rest.

Anna was bearing an apple pie, a gift from her mother. As soon as she had handed it over, she asked in her high reedy voice if "the boy" was in. She wanted to see him.

Hidden beneath the weeping willow, Joshua put his head on his knees and blocked his ears. His mother would call him, he knew. She had to do what the girl said. And he didn't want to hear.

Surprisingly, his mother said he was out; she needn't have bothered, for Anna found him all by herself and arrived, flush-faced and triumphant, through the curtain of fronds, just as he was waiting for the gate to close behind her.

He stared at her. "Go!" he said finally. "You mustn't stay here."

"Why not?"

"Because you cannot play with me."

"Why not?"

Well, why not? He could not explain. Instead, he mutely held out his own black wrist and laid it by her white one, so she could see the contrast.

She stared down at them and then at him. A faint inkling dawned, he could see.

"But my mummy doesn't mind. Really she doesn't!"

Joshua rolled his eyes, began to put both hands up as if to surrender, then broke and ran. He did not look back, but as he rounded the corner of the house, he heard the gate clash to.

He spent the rest of the afternoon in the cupboard under the stairs.

Chapter Ten

That night something woke Joshua. He lay in bed listening, holding his breath, half stifled in the blankets, holding the edge in his fingertips and rubbing it back and forth while his eyes and ears strained at the darkness.

It was no good. He wouldn't sleep again now. He slipped out of the bed, careful not to disturb his mother, and stood frozen for a moment.

The room was very dark. He thought of the *tokolosh,* the little evil spirit that haunted bedrooms. The *tokolosh* was too short to reach the bed, said Beauty, as long as it was up on bricks. Still—he gulped and ran out of the room.

Outside, the moon hung low and yellow, wringing odd shadows from the trees along the path. There was a plash from the pool and a deep slow murmur of voices. He tiptoed from shadow to shadow until he saw them, sitting by the humming filtration tank. There was an air of contained excitement.

Just as he hesitated, hanging back behind the fig tree,

they saw him. There was a silence and a pleased murmur, and then another silence as he came among them.

He went to each, despite his shyness, and greeted them as he had been taught, with a respectful bob of the head. Then he leaned against Tsumalo. The men were quiet. Eventually, one of them said: "The boy. We could use the boy. He could take messages."

"No!" said Tsumalo. "It is safer if he does not know anything."

Joshua stood quiet, pressed against him, eyes down; he was trembling. His heart leaped, a single bound, then thumped slowly and loudly in his chest.

"There is trouble coming soon," said one of the men. He was small and narrow, with a thin face like a fox's. "The government says that our children must be taught all their subjects in Afrikaans," he explained, looking at Joshua. "Why should they want that? It is bound to make them do worse in their exams."

Joshua didn't reply. At home he had been taught in Xhosa.

There was no more talk of messages. The murmuring continued, and Tsumalo wrote in his notebook; finally, the men melted away into the grayness of the predawn.

Joshua ran back to his mother's room. She was stirring. The Madam and the Master took their tea at seven sharp: weak, with a slice of lemon, for the Madam; strong, with hot milk, for the Master.

He sighed and shivered to convince his mother he had just been out in the cold for a pee, then slipped back into the space she had vacated, pulling the covers up high over his head and breathing in the warmth luxuriously.

Beauty did not talk much about Tsumalo, though she prepared his meals along with hers and the gardener's, and every few days she went down to the shed and dressed his wounds. Gradually the leg became a little less swollen and the bruises began to heal; Tsumalo had to walk slowly, using the stick for balance.

Joshua could tell she worried that Mr. Malherbe — so sensitive about how much milk was drunk in his kitchen — would notice that more food was being eaten.

But white households were extravagant places. Joshua saw more food consumed in a day than his Ciskei family ate in a week. At any rate, little was said, though Goodman came in one day and asked flatly, "When is he going?"

"I don't know. How can I know?" Beauty shrugged her plump shoulders. "He can't go with that leg. Not yet."

"It is no good. It is not safe."

Goodman's voice was pitched low; he was standing at the back door with his plate and mug in his hands, turning and turning them as he spoke.

Beauty took them, and they stood close at the door, murmuring.

"*Aaai,* no, it is not true!" She broke away suddenly and disappeared into the kitchen. Joshua, who had been trying to hear the conversation, carried on with his task of pegging up the washing on the lines that stretched across the yard.

That night he woke and found the bed cold beside him,

the sheet smooth. His heart leaped in his throat, and he jumped out of bed with no thought for the *tokolosh*.

He ran down the windy path to the shed. The low creepers grabbed at him. He saw the light in the window; he forgot to whistle and banged on the door with both fists. There was a shriek from inside. Tsumalo opened the door a crack.

"It is only you," he said. He sounded relieved. Joshua was unable to speak. Then, "Mama! Mama!" he sobbed.

Tsumalo slowly opened the door. Beauty looked at him sorrowfully from the bed. She opened her arms to him.

"I just came to talk to Tsumalo," she said. "I am going to ask my friend to look at his leg. She works at the children's hospital. I am worried it is taking too long to heal."

Joshua and Beauty returned to their room, but every night after that he woke again and again through the night, checking that she was still there.

He thought about the twins; he missed them a lot. Xola was plump and tough, but he cried just as much as Phumla when Beauty left.

He recalled Phumla's narrow face and anxious eyes, her thin body clinging fiercely to their mother's legs as they said good-bye that last time. Everyone was crying: his grandmother, the twins, the baby; the truck tooted and rocked in the dusty road as the driver played with brake and clutch to let them know it was time to go. All these things he pondered, looking into the darkness, hugging his mother so tightly that she hissed and shrugged him off, but sleepily, so he didn't mind.

Chapter Eleven

Suddenly, everything was changing. Mrs. Malherbe arrived in the kitchen like a whirlwind, hissing and fussing, her elbows out like an angry hen in a dust patch.

The sheets in the guest room were to be changed. The room was to be spring-cleaned. The lawn was to be mowed and edged—that very day! *But it's Wednesday,* thought Joshua. Wednesday was the day the flower beds were weeded.

He felt breathless and stood back against the chimney breast, by the side of the big stove. Mr. Malherbe was away, so it was safe to be in the kitchen. But today he didn't feel safe.

"You!" Her lean, dried-out, angry face was right up close. Her eyes were pale blue with wrinkles cut deep into the skin around them. "You can make yourself useful for a change. I want that pool vacuumed properly this time. And I want the filter basket cleared out. Do you hear me?"

He nodded mutely.

Goodman mowed the lawn with his shoulders hunched

over, a sign that he was angry. The flower beds would get out of hand. Then who would be in trouble?

Joshua stood at the side of the pool, struggling with the length and heft of the vacuum pole. You had to push it just right, very, very gently and slowly, or the dust would rise from the bottom of the pool and hang in obstinate clouds. Too slowly and it would take forever. He would still be here, at the shallow end, when Mrs. Malherbe's son arrived this afternoon at four o'clock.

And the dead frogs would still be bobbing in the filter basket. The lemons would still be on the tree. He tried to remember all the things he still had to do, and, frowning, he pushed just a little too hard. The pole shot out of his hand and jittered across the pool.

He let it clatter against the side and ran to the lemon tree. He picked three of the biggest fruits, ran to the kitchen, and put them in the bowl. Then he ran back to the pool, squeezed his eyes shut, stuck his hand in deep, and lifted out the basket with its quota of green bodies and dumped them, without looking, on the compost heap.

By the time he got back, the dust had settled. He picked up the pole and resumed his slow sweep across the floor of the pool.

Later, from his perch in the loquat tree, he heard a car arrive with a deep throaty roar: it was a bright red sports car, with the top down. He saw the gate open, and a head of springy, curly brown hair, and a hand holding a battered carryall.

The doorbell went, the front door flew open, and Mrs.

Malherbe came out. Joshua had never seen her smile so. She held on to the young man as if her arms would break with the holding.

"Robert, Robert," was all she said.

Robert smiled too. "You're looking well, Ma." But as they turned together on the porch, Joshua could see the concern in his eyes. Mrs. Malherbe was thinner than ever. Her eyes were purple with shadows.

They went inside.

It seemed that Mr. Malherbe was away for longer than usual. Joshua always loved his absences; Mrs. Malherbe relaxed and so did the staff.

This time, though, it was the arrival of Robert that made it seem like a holiday. He teased Beauty and sought out Goodman and told him the garden had never looked better. He threw Joshua up in the air, terrifying him, and laughed until the boy laughed too.

Then he found Tsumalo. Normally visitors didn't venture to the bottom of the garden. But Robert remembered the shed from when he was a child himself and went to find it. Tsumalo leaped to his feet in terror, he later told Joshua. He had thought the game was up.

But then Robert had talked to him. Robert had said he should call him Robert. Not Master or Mister Robert. Robert could be trusted, said Tsumalo.

Joshua wasn't so sure, though it was hard not to like Robert. Even Mrs. Malherbe looked happier when he was around. But he was a white man. Like Mr. Malherbe. You never knew what they could do. What if he told?

Chapter Twelve

Evening; his special place again. He had a digestive biscuit with him, just the one; he shared it with Betsy, straight down the middle. His mother was serving the meal, and he immediately noticed the difference: Mrs. Malherbe's voice was raised and lilting, Robert's laugh came deep through the walls, and even his mother laughed, a giggle that was almost too quiet to hear.

Then his mother washed up and left, and Joshua heard it: the sudden change in Robert's voice as the back door shut.

"You can't go on like this."

A pause. "No."

"Then leave him."

"I can't."

"You must."

Another hesitation. "I can't. You must see that."

Robert's voice rose again. "He's a bastard."

Her voice was bitter. "Yes."

"Don't you think he might stop if I talk to him? Even bastards must have some compassion."

Compassion. This was a word Joshua had never heard. He strained to hear more. His belly felt tight across the top, as though he had eaten something that disagreed with him, or had put on a belt that was much too small.

He had heard her getting sick. Babies made you sick. Was she going to have a baby? He knew you must not hit a woman who was having a baby or she might lose it.

He listened. They had gone quiet. Then he realized it was just the silence before she began to cry: harsh, racking sobs.

He curled himself into the smallest ball he could and hugged the dog, stroking her long ears. He buried his head in the soft folds of basset skin around her neck. He was crying too, and he didn't know why.

In the morning Mrs. Malherbe's MG was gone. So were Mrs. Malherbe and Robert. Joshua stood silently sweeping the pool, frowning, watching the floor clear of dust in clean stripes. He felt he was only just beginning to learn how to do it. The sun was shimmering at the rusty edges of the poplar leaves.

He couldn't see him, but he felt that Tsumalo was standing beside him.

"How's it?" he asked.

"OK." Tsumalo rested a hand on his shoulder, but gently, so as not to disturb the quiet rhythm of his sweeping.

"I think they are at the hospital. The car is gone."

"Mmmmh." Tsumalo didn't say another word. Together they stood and watched as the vacuum passed back and forth, wiping out the dirt, sucking out the bad, leaving only the good, clean blue floor of the pool.

Still silent, Tsumalo went for the pool net. He scooped out the leaves while Joshua cleared the filter basket. No frogs; just more leaves. The summer was on the turn. As the man twisted the pole, twisted and turned, emptying the glistening piles on the crazy paving, Joshua shivered. The leaves looked burned, misshapen, drowned.

But soon the pool was its limpid self again, glittering in the sunlight, keeping itself to itself, holding its secrets like a magic looking-glass in a story.

Tsumalo picked up his stick and left; Joshua began to lift the piles of wet leaves into a wheelbarrow.

Then Mrs. Malherbe and Robert were back. Her MG came into the driveway with the bump and scrape that meant it was loaded down, and she and Robert were laughing and unloading the trunk.

They brought out bags and bags. All colors, and stuffed with what looked like clothes and presents.

So they hadn't been to the hospital. They had been shopping. Joshua had been thinking all day of Mrs. Malherbe, and now she was laughing.

Chapter Thirteen

R obert's cheerful face appeared around the hedge that hid the pool from the garden. "Hey, you! Come on in!"

Joshua hesitated. Had he done something wrong?

"Come on! The Madam's waiting for you!" Robert grinned at him. His curly hair fell forward as he shook his head. "What are you waiting for?"

Joshua took the net gently from the pool and laid it on the crazy paving. He followed Robert up the steps to the side veranda and into the house. He'd never been in the living room before, and he stood awkwardly on the parquet just inside the door.

The sofas were huge and pink, with curly wooden legs. There were two wing chairs by the fireplace, great falls of cream curtain touching the floor, and in the center of the patterned carpet, a pile of shopping bags, with brightly colored tissue paper spilling out.

"Well, boy, what are you waiting for?" asked Mrs. Malherbe. She was sitting in one of the wing chairs with a large gin and tonic in her hand. Smiling.

He felt a little clutch of anxiety. He had never seen her smile in this way before. The smile reached her eyes, and her thin face was glowing.

He didn't know what to do. Robert laughed, waded into the pile, and handed him a brightly striped sweater.

He looked at it. It must be for—whom? Did Robert have children? He didn't think so.

"Try it on! It's for you!" Robert was laughing at him.

His face grew hot. He pulled it on over his head. For a moment the blood roared in his ears. He could hear nothing but the beat of his own skin and smell the slight chlorine smell of himself, the himself who had been quietly dipping and scooping the net into the dimpled pool, alone. The way he liked it.

Then Robert was pulling the sweater down, smiling at him, and spinning him around by the shoulders.

"Just look at him, Ma! He's a new boy!"

Mrs. Malherbe raised her glass to him. It was empty, he noticed. She smiled again, but the merriment had left her eyes. She waved carelessly at the rest of the clothes. "Take them," she said. "They're all for you. You don't have to try them on here. Let me know if any of them don't fit."

"Thank you, Madam," Joshua said, bobbing his head.

"Robert—get me another one?" She held out the glass.

He carried the folded clothing carefully back to the room in one of the big bags. It had STUTTAFORDS written on the side in big curly dark green letters.

He thought his mother would be angry with him, although he wasn't sure why. But she wasn't. She said nothing, just took the clothes from him and ran her hands over the T-shirts, the sweaters, the corduroy trousers with cuffs, the long khaki shorts.

She put them away in the drawers. There was plenty of space: he had only two pairs of patched shorts, two secondhand, long-sleeved shirts, and a sweater. Then she went across the yard and into the house, though it was her afternoon rest time.

Later he found out that she had gone to Mrs. Malherbe and said, "Madam, I will pay you for the clothes. You can take it out of my wages."

Mrs. Malherbe and Robert had laughed. She had said, "No, Beauty. They are a present. Your son works in the garden. He's a good boy. We don't like to see him wearing those ragged clothes."

Or so his mother told him. What they did not understand was that the gift itself was a kind of insult, a wound that went so deep that Beauty could not express it.

Joshua understood, and when she told him, he hugged her hard and said in a muffled voice against her shoulder, "We can give them back. I don't need them."

But she pushed him away and said, her voice rough with fatigue, "No. We will keep them. It is like they are giving you wages for your work. It is fair."

He thought he would not wear the clothes, out of loyalty to her, but after a few days he put on one of the T-shirts.

Then he pulled out the new shorts and ran his hands over them. They were so soft!

Beauty came back into the room and saw him. "You must wear them," she said. "Otherwise the Madam will be upset."

He helped his mother in the house. Once a week she did a big cleaning in the kitchen, and on those days he would climb the stairs with their wide polished banisters to collect the dirty clothes and damp towels from the floors of the bathrooms, the dressing room, and the bedrooms.

Joshua stood in front of Mrs. Malherbe's long oval mirror, wearing the long-sleeved khaki shirt and shorts. He had never bothered with mirrors before. But he looked grown-up now, he thought: serious.

He gazed deep into his own eyes. They were dark brown, like his mother's, with veins in the white parts. He had a long face, with a dimple on one side when he smiled, but his mother's face was broad, with high slanted cheekbones. He wondered what his father's looked like.

He glanced down at his hands and turned them over slowly. They were dark on the backs and light on the palms. Why was that? He turned them again, considering. Aside from the darker creases across them, his palms could almost pass for white. But he couldn't. His coppery darkness meant he lived in the dark. In the back of the white house. Under the stairs. In the backyard. Down at the bottom of the garden. At the bottom of the heap.

These clothes made him feel different. Just like a darker,

smaller version of Robert. He had legs and arms, like Robert. Teeth that were even and white. Strong hands. But would he ever drive a car like Robert's? Would he ever be so happy?

He heard a footstep on the stairs, grabbed an armful of washing from the floor, and dashed for the back stairs, his heart beating fast.

Chapter Fourteen

It was morning; bright and cold. Joshua ran across the yard, came into the kitchen, and stopped. His mother and the gardener were standing, looking at the radio on the windowsill. Goodman never came beyond the back door. And even more astonishing, Tsumalo was leaning against the doorjamb, holding a tin mug.

The radio was saying something that Joshua could not understand. Something about stones. Something about schoolchildren. Something about shooting.

"Mama, what—" he began urgently.

"Sssst!" They all turned on him.

Then the man stopped talking. Beauty turned off the radio. There was silence among them.

"Aaai," said Beauty. "It is no good." She was trembling.

"It is what we want. It is the only thing." It was Tsumalo. He crossed the room and clattered his mug into the sink. "You want to stay as you are?"

He looked scornfully at Goodman, who said nothing, just looked at the floor.

"I am afraid," said Beauty.

"Afraid!" His face was close to hers. "What is there to be afraid of? The worst thing has already happened. And it has happened to you."

His forehead shone with sweat, and there was a tiny bubble of foam at the corner of his mouth.

"The worst thing is how we live. Like animals. Like oxen for the plow. Like beasts! When they don't want us anymore, they can shoot us. Just like they shot Sipho!"

Joshua felt a fist close hard about his heart. His mother flew across the room and held him, as if that could erase what he had just heard. But it was too late.

Sipho. Sipho. He tore himself away and ran out of the kitchen, down the path, into the shrubbery. When Tsumalo found him, he was up the oak tree, fist stuffed in his mouth, tears streaming down his face. Sipho.

Tsumalo reached up and laid his heavy hand on Joshua's back. "I am sorry. I should not have said. I thought you knew."

Joshua said nothing. Streams of snot ran down from his nose, and he scrubbed at them with his new khaki sleeve.

"Your brother was a hero. He died"—Joshua gasped and cried out for the first time—"he died fighting the police. But remember, he was a hero. Because of people like him"— Tsumalo grasped Joshua's resisting form in his arms—"you and I will be free one day."

Joshua wriggled from Tsumalo's hold, dropped to the ground, and ran again. Tsumalo did not follow him.

Chapter Fifteen

Mr. Malherbe was still away in Jo'burg on business, and soon Robert had to go too, the red Alfa chuntering up the road, and the house returned to its usual torpor, basking in the winter sunlight, the sound of Beauty's polisher whining over the floorboards.

Betsy swam in the pool and made them laugh, solemnly treading a circle with her huge paws, her ears spread out on the water beside her.

There were no more news reports.

Joshua cried in the night for Sipho. Beauty shushed him gently, half asleep, turning and holding him close; he could feel her own body shaking with suppressed sobs. "I am sorry that I did not tell you about Sipho," she told him in the dark. "You are still so young. I did not want you to grieve for him."

One morning he got up early and tiptoed across the yard to get her a proper cup of tea. But as he stood on the red-polished *stoep*, fitting the Yale key in the door, he thought he heard a heavy tread inside the house. Mr. Malherbe. He ran back, thudding into the bed with his feet cold from the yellow dust of the yard.

He lay in the half-light, listening to the doves practicing uncertainly in the trees. Then Beauty began to stir, and he got up to put on the Calor gas ring to boil water. He would have to use an old tea bag from the night before. He put sweet Carnation milk in the cup and brought it to her, the steam spiraling in the cold air.

"I went to bring you real tea," he said. "But I heard the Master."

She smiled at him and put her hand softly on his head, then took the cup and drank. "He is still away," she said.

Later, as he ate cornflakes and milk on the back step, he heard strange stuttering roars in the distance, with gaps in between. It seemed to be coming from near the Red Cross children's hospital at the side of the common.

He didn't like the noise. It seemed to make the house shake. It sounded like big guns. He put the bowl down, stood, and looked toward the back of the yard, in the direction of the big square of open ground where the children's hospital stood on one side and the white girls' school on the other.

He went back into the kitchen. "What is this noise?" he asked her.

"It is only the roadworks," she said. "They are drilling the road to make it wider." She checked the wall clock and switched on the radio. They sat down at the table.

The green baize door swung and swung on its hinges. Mrs. Malherbe swept into the room and stopped, her attention caught by the pips on the hour. Slowly, she pulled out a chair and sat down, chin propped on her arms, eyes fixed on the sunlit yard wall by Beauty's room with its tracery of vine branches. When the bulletin finished, she twisted the dial to zero and stood up.

"From tonight, and until the Master comes home," she said, "you are to sleep in the house. You and the boy"—and she nodded at Joshua.

"Make up a bed in the back spare room. And I want Goodman to put extra bolts on the doors. The side doors too and the swing door. Betsy will have to sleep out here. She can take her chances. We should have a proper dog."

It was strange to be in this big room. The walls were the green of a Granny Smith apple in the half-light. The ceiling was high and all around the edge it had a pattern, like the complicated curls on the sides of a cake. In the middle there was a circle, with little creamy scallops, where the light hung. The curtains moved a little at the bay window. The streetlight shone onto the ceiling.

Joshua's eyes began to close, though he fought sleep. His mother was still downstairs, cleaning up, and he wanted to stay awake until she came upstairs. He wished Betsy was up here too, snoring comfortably in her basket. The upstairs was so quiet, with its big dark rooms off the wide corridor. He could hear Mrs. Malherbe in her room. A drawer banged shut.

He clenched all his muscles and grasped the blanket's nubbled edge in his fists. He would not fall asleep. He would not. He would not.

A sound woke him. Car lights ran across the ceiling, and the rattle of the engine told him it was a diesel.

Then another noise. He slid out of bed and hopped from the cold floorboards to the rug. He stood at the window and looked down at the garden.

At its far end, the floodlights flicked on, and it was washed in a lurid green light. The pool swam, blue as an extra sky, behind its hedges. A movement caught his eye beyond the filtration tank. The lights were doused, and suddenly he understood.

This time it was different. The silence was heavy. When they saw him, a little sigh ran around them like a breeze.

Then: "They were children," said one. "Kids like him."

"*Amabhulu zizinja.* The Boers are dogs, to kill children." Another voice came out of the darkness.

Joshua felt Tsumalo's hand on his shoulder. "This boy," said Tsumalo. "His brother was killed. They shot him like a wild beast."

"Sipho," he added the name softly. "His name was Sipho."

"*Amabhulu zizinja.*"

"*Amabhulu zizinja.*"

"*Amabhulu zizinja.*"

"Go to bed now," said Tsumalo. "This is no place for you."

"*Hamba kahle, boetie.* Go well."

"Go well."

"Go well."

In the morning, his mother was not in the bed beside him.

She was in the kitchen, making the tea. The radio was on, playing soft music, and tears were running straight down her plump cheeks.

"*Hayi,*" she said. "*Hayi.* It is not right. All those children!" And she hugged him hard. He felt her body quaking. He was frightened. She wouldn't let him go. She was hurting him. He squirmed.

Mrs. Malherbe came in, and they broke apart. Normally, she would have glared and said: "Beauty, where is my tea? You know I like it at seven sharp."

But she didn't say anything; she just crossed to the radio and turned it up as the pips came on. She stirred the teapot, poured two cups, and put one on the table in front of Beauty. She poured a glass of milk, handed it to Joshua, and sat down heavily.

They listened in silence.

The doorbell rang. Beauty began to get up.

"No — I'll go," said Mrs. Malherbe.

They heard her say, "Who is it?" They heard the bolts slide and the heavy door shift over the thick hall carpet.

Then she was back. Robert was with her. His shirt was torn at the shoulder, there was a bloody gash on his arm, and his face was bruised. He leaned heavily on the table and sat down carefully.

"What happened?" Mrs. Malherbe whispered. Her face was suffused with color; it ran in a mottled rash down her neck.

"There were riots in Guguletu," he said brusquely. "Haven't you heard?"

Mrs. Malherbe shook her head. She hugged herself with one arm, and pressed her fist to her mouth.

Beauty filled an enamel basin with water and brought it to the table. Joshua fetched the first-aid kit. Then he stood by the door while Mrs. Malherbe cut away Robert's sleeve and swabbed at the blood. It floated in the water.

"It was a massacre," said Robert, and waved at his arm. "Whites spend their lives worrying about Armageddon. Well, it's here. It's bloody well here. Only not for us." He slammed his good hand on the table.

"Hold still," Mrs. Malherbe said. "Or I'll never get this finished." Her tone was brisk; her color had returned. She wrapped a bandage over the cotton and gauze, pulling it tight and securing it with tape.

Robert drew in his breath sharply. "I need to file," he said. "I need a table, a typewriter, and a phone. I can't get back to the office. Ma?" Mrs. Malherbe nodded.

Robert's blue eyes found Joshua's, and he scrabbled in his pockets and tossed a jingling bundle at him along with a smile. "The car's in the drive. Clean it up for me? It's caught a couple of rocks. Luckily the windshield's survived."

"Thanks," he added over his shoulder as he left the room.

69

Chapter Sixteen

The typing stopped and started; stopped and started. Then the clattering halted and they could hear Robert talking on the phone. Finally, he was finished.

He appeared at the kitchen door. "I'm famished," he said. "And I've missed your food, Beauty. Any chance of something to eat?"

"The lunch, it will be ready soon, Master Robert." Beauty looked up from the carrots she was chopping into coins and smiled at him. Joshua watched from the red stool by the stove. She never smiled at Mr. and Mrs. Malherbe.

"How is the Master's arm?"

"Oh, Beauty. Please don't call me 'Master.'" And he smiled back at her. "How's Tsumalo? Still here?" Robert helped himself to a beer from the pot-bellied Frigidaire, flipped off the cap against the counter's metal edge, and took a swallow.

"Yes, Master. He is still here. It has been a good hiding place."

"What a joke. Do you know how long they have been looking for him? He is a famous man, your Tsumalo. There is graffiti on De Waal Drive. It says, 'Viva Ngenge, Tsumalo is King.' They think he is in Maputo." Robert laughed, delighted.

Joshua went to look through the porthole in the green baize door.

"*Sssst!* The Madam, she is coming!" Panic caught at his voice.

Robert picked up Mrs. Malherbe's gin and tonic from the table and went through the swing door without a pause.

"Let's sit on the *stoep*," they heard him say. "Hard to believe it's winter; it's so warm outside."

It was after supper. Robert leaned against the red Formica counter with a mug of coffee while Beauty washed up. "So where's Tsumalo—out holding a meeting?" It was a joke, Joshua thought. Tsumalo could not go anywhere far, although the leg was less swollen and his limp less pronounced. Joshua had begun to smuggle books from Mr. Malherbe's study out to the shed.

Tsumalo had begun by laughing. The first book Joshua found for him was by George Adamson. "Look. *Born Free,*" he had said, holding up the book with the bearded man and the lioness on the cover. "That's me. Born to be free."

But when Joshua brought him books by Marx and Orwell and Huxley, he stopped laughing and went silent as he looked at them, though he threw the Kipling against the wall—"Racist pig!" he said—and laughed at the school history book. "Look," he said. "Simon van der Stel. He was the first Dutch governor of the Cape. And do you know what? He was Colored. But does it say that here? No, it doesn't."

71

"You must be careful," Joshua said. "I must put them back." He picked up the Kipling and the dark gray *History of South Africa, Standard 9–10,* with its paper covers. He smoothed them down and crept back into the house with them. He waited until Mrs. Malherbe had gone to bed and then slipped them back onto the study shelves, exactly where they had come from. Always in alphabetical order. He knew his ABCs. He was OK.

But no one ever noticed. If Mr. Malherbe had once read the books, he certainly didn't anymore. When he was home, he sat in the study with his whiskey after dinner, falling asleep over the newspaper. He never glanced at the shelves. There were rows and rows of orange-backed books with black penguins on the spines. Joshua tried to read them sometimes, struggling over the words; he smuggled them out to the room so his mother could read with him.

"I was lucky," she told him. "I went to a mission school. They were good teachers. Now I am glad because I can read with you."

Joshua liked to borrow the old Enid Blytons on the bottom shelf. They were easy to read, though the world she wrote about was strange. There was a girl called George. And a boy called Julian. There was danger but it was only pretend danger, angry men who did not ever do anything really bad, and picnics by the sea, and parents at the end, and safety, and cocoa, and a dog called Timmy.

There were never policemen who beat you for no reason. There were never adults who behaved inexplicably. There was never, ever murder, blood, or death.

Oh, the stories he could tell! He had learned most of them from his grandmother, but he liked to embellish them with extra bits. He told them to Tsumalo sometimes, sitting in the shed at night, talking with a little candle stuck on the packing case at the end of the bed.

". . . And then they ran away to the mountains and lived on *suurvygies* and eucalyptus leaves and baked tortoise forever and ever and ever."

How Tsumalo laughed! He took Joshua's head in his hands and gazed at him and said: "If I ever have a son, I want him to be just like you!"

But sometimes Tsumalo would want to lie and read quietly, and he would shake his head and say, "Yes, yes!" to himself, and Joshua would be forced to read the comics that he had already read: *Superman* and *Batman and Robin, Richie Rich* and *Archie and Veronica.* He liked Veronica. He thought she was like Anna. She was so mean. He thought he would like to be like that — then no one would ever dare to be mean to him.

Other times, Tsumalo would make him read aloud. It was supposed to be good for him. "If you are going to be a free man, you must know how to read well," said Tsumalo. "It is the most important thing in the world. If you can read, you can teach yourself anything. Anything!"

And he would stop and gaze out the window of the shed with its tacked-on flowered curtain that Beauty had made, and narrow his eyes and say dreamily, "Yes, you must learn how to read like a white boy."

Chapter Seventeen

Mummy says you're going to kill us all."

Joshua turned around. He had the polish and cloth in his hand. He couldn't see where the voice was coming from, but he knew it was Anna's. He put the tin down carefully by Robert's car. Was she in the tree?

"Over here, you *moegoe!*" But he still couldn't see her.

"*Pssst!*"

He looked at the fence. He could see the knothole. Nothing.

He shrugged, picked up the tin, and dolloped some of the pink gunk onto the red hood of the Alfa. There was a jagged hole in its smooth surface. He would have to be careful.

He could feel the outrage coming from behind him, and he smiled to himself as he spread the polish.

There was a hot breath at his elbow. He looked down at Anna. He hadn't realized how small she was. She was wearing a striped T-shirt that failed to quite meet the waistband of her shorts, exposing a creamy roll of flesh.

"Hey," he said. "Where's your pretty dress?"

"I hate dresses! I'm a tomboy!"

He handed her the cloth without comment and went to get another. As he rounded the corner of the house, she called after him: "Hey, boy!"

He turned.

"Are you? Going to kill us all?"

"Not if you polish that car properly!" he said. He was impressed at his own daring.

Robert was coming down the back stairs from the *stoep*. "Hey, how're you doing? How's that car coming?" The blue eyes were blurry, Joshua could see. There was a beer in his hand. "Where's Tsumalo?"

"I don't know, Master," said Joshua, giving the little bob of respect he'd been taught.

"Don't call me Master!" Robert laughed. "Let no man call me Master . . ." He weaved off down the path. Joshua watched him negotiate the gate into the garden unsteadily, bottle dangling from his fingertips.

"Why are they smashing up the schools?" asked Anna. "It's silly." She was folding and refolding her cloth, watching Joshua as he finished the intricacies of the wheel spokes with his cloth-wrapped finger.

Joshua shrugged. He didn't want to talk. Since the news about Sipho, since the radio bulletins, since Robert had returned from Guguletu, he'd felt — ragged. Torn inside. Shaky. He was angry. Those poor children! How could grown men shoot them? Didn't they have children of their own?

That moment when he had stood in front of the mirror

seemed a lifetime ago. He had felt different then. He had felt . . . He realized Anna was looking at him, waiting for an answer.

"How must I know!" he exploded. "How must I know!"

"We give them schools, we give them books, and this is how they repay us," she said in a singsong voice. She had obviously heard her parents talking. "But where would they be without us?"

She gave him a sly look. "Is that what you think?"

He rubbed furiously at the shining wheel, not looking at her.

"I must go in now," he said. "The car is finished. I have other work to do."

And he held out his hand for her cloth.

Normally, she would have said, "Can I help you?" Normally, she would have said, "Oh, please let me. *Pleeease*," and turned down her mouth, and her face would have flushed dark red. Normally, she would have trailed behind him, whining.

Today she handed him the cloth and went.

Joshua sat on the filtration tank, kicking his heels. He did not know what to do. He'd cleaned the pool. He did not have any other jobs left. His mother, he knew, had gone to visit her friend Hester at Anna's house. Although she was only next door, he couldn't go there.

Anna could come here as much as she liked. But then, she could go anywhere, he thought. She went to school every day. She could go to the beach. She could go to the shops.

She could ride that smart new bike of hers up and down the road. She could go to the top of Table Mountain. She could sit on those benches that said SLEGS BLANKES. WHITES ONLY. She could ride on any bus she chose. Only she'd be driven in her father's big black Jaguar with the leaping silver cat on the front of the hood.

And when she was grown up? She would have a choice. She could be a white Madam like Mrs. Malherbe—only younger, he couldn't imagine her that old—and have white brats like the Websters across the road, and run her finger along the mantelpiece and say to her maid, "What's this? I pay you to keep the house clean." Or she could go to university and be a doctor. She could go overseas. She could do anything.

And him? What could he do? He could just about read, thanks to his mother and Tsumalo. He might, if he was lucky, go back to school one day. Then, when he was grown up, he might get a job in the mines, like Sipho. Or be a gardener like Goodman.

If he was unlucky, he would end up as a *bergie*, sleeping rough on the mountain, drinking purple meths, the cheapest alcohol there was. Which would kill him, eventually.

He jumped off the tank and headed up the path toward Tsumalo's shed. He was angry.

He saw Robert coming down the path toward him, Robert with his blue eyes and his wide grin and his curly hair, looking more unsteady now, but even friendlier.

Joshua turned his face the other way and ran straight past. He had to talk to Tsumalo.

77

Chapter Eighteen

When he got to the shed, Tsumalo was staring out the window. He was smoking, something Joshua had never seen him do.

"Tsumalo! I have to talk to you! Why have the riots happened? What is going on?"

"Hey," said Tsumalo. It was a very small cigarette, hand-rolled.

"Tsumalo! Why did they kill all those children?"

But the man was in a strange mood. "It is all going according to plan," he said tersely. "They won't be in power for much longer. The people will rise up."

He didn't want to talk; Joshua lay stretched beside him on the bed, Tsumalo's arm around him.

"That Robert," said Tsumalo. "What a man. He's going to make me famous."

"Famous?" asked Joshua, puzzled.

"Yeah. He's done an interview with me. And it's going to be in the *Guardian*."

"What do you mean, the guardian?" asked Joshua.

Tsumalo sighed. "It's a great newspaper in England." And he looked again out the little window, with its flowered curtain and the view of the emaciated poplar trees moving back and forth, back and forth.

"In England," repeated Joshua. England was overseas, he knew that. And in England they wanted South Africa to come right. They thought it was unfair that there were no votes for black people. That much he had learned from Tsumalo.

He pondered for a moment. Before Tsumalo came, he had not even known what a vote was.

"So—that's good, right?"

Tsumalo laughed. "Do you know—they have written on the walls of our city about me? I am already famous. Hey . . ." And he looked away again, drawing on the spliff.

"I know," said Joshua. "'Viva Ngenge,'" he repeated. "'Tsumalo is King.' They think you are in Maputo. Where is Maputo?" he asked. "Is it near England?"

Tsumalo laughed out loud and hugged him hard. "Hey," he said into his ear. "You are better than a son, you know that?"

Joshua felt a small squeeze of anxiety in his stomach. If he was like a son, then Tsumalo was like a father. And this father too might disappear.

"Hey," said Tsumalo. "Don't hug me so hard. That hurts."

He rubbed his thumb across the boy's cheeks. "Now off you go back to your mother. Or she will be worried."

Joshua nodded mutely and ran. It was almost suppertime. Although he was hungry, his tummy felt as if it had gone into a knot, and he could not eat, though it was roast chicken, his favorite.

Would Tsumalo go away like his father? Or rather, not like his father; he had spent time with Tsumalo, and he had never really known his father.

His father had another wife, his mother had told him, a city wife. He never sent money for Joshua and his brothers and sister. That's why his mother had to leave them—all except Joshua—with her own parents, in the Ciskei, and come to Cape Town to earn a living. She had to earn enough to send money back for their keep, for their school fees, for their uniforms, for their books.

That was why she had the knitting machine. With it, she made jerseys in the evenings for other people's children. She could earn more money that way.

Mrs. Malherbe, she told him, bought many of them to give as gifts to her nieces and nephews, for their little children.

Beauty had found a box of them in the attic one day. And when she told the Madam, the Madam had said quickly, "Oh, Beauty, they have grown out of them now. Do you think you can sell them? It would be a pity to waste them."

Beauty did not believe the Madam. "She must have forgotten to send them," she told Joshua, a frown creasing her forehead.

"But it was very kind of her to buy them from me. And to give them back. Now I can sell them to my friends."

So Mrs. Malherbe wasn't so bad, then. Joshua wondered

why she was so sharp with Beauty. Perhaps it was because she was unhappy.

After supper, he said he would wash up. He wanted to cuddle with Betsy in his secret place. He hadn't been there for a while, and he wanted a little solitude. He needed to think.

Chapter Nineteen

When Joshua went upstairs, Beauty was already asleep. She had one hand curled under her cheek. She looked peaceful; almost happy. He slipped in beside her.

This room was so comfortable. It was cold in the mornings, but the asbestos heater soon warmed it up. There was a thick rug on the floor. There was even a hand basin in the corner. The blankets and sheets in here smelled cleaner too; they weren't musty and damp. There was no peeling plaster and no smell of paraffin, no scratching of mice behind the walls.

Oh, the mice. In his mother's room, they had woken once and found the bag of sugar nibbled at the corner. All the white sugar had run out onto the floor, and there were little mouse tracks in it. And tiny strings of mouse poo, like black beads. After that, they got a tin for the sugar.

They still had to use the maid's bathroom, though. It was in the corner of the courtyard, behind the clotheslines. It was always freezing in there, and the hot water, piped across from the main house, was lukewarm by the time it dribbled into the rust-stained bath.

It was the same bath that they washed Betsy in.

The rain began, thrumming against the windows, rushing through the gutters, and to its comforting sound, he fell asleep.

There was something wrong. He could feel it as soon as he woke. Beauty still breathed quietly beside him, hand under her cheek, her wide mouth curved up at the corners.

The streetlight shone in. The rain had stopped, and the house was quiet.

He held his breath. The kitchen was below them; he thought he could hear a chair leg shift on the linoleum. And then a murmur, a voice. No: two voices.

He padded down the stairs. At the baize door, he hesitated: he was too short to see through its porthole. He crept into the dining room; it had a door into the back hall. This he opened a crack. Betsy woke and looked at him; he put his hand up, telling her to stay where she was. She put her head down on her paws again, looking up at him from her wrinkly, red-rimmed eyes.

He strained to hear. The voices belonged to Mrs. Malherbe and, although it seemed incredible, to Tsumalo. What could he possibly say to her? What could she say to him? Why hadn't she called the police? Then he heard a third voice. Of course. Robert.

"I know it looks bad, Ma," he said. "But it's the safest place for him. Nobody is looking for him here. And it's only till they come for him in a couple of days. Then he'll be leaving the country, and you'll never see him again."

"You know very well how I feel," came Mrs. Malherbe's dry voice. "You have your right to your beliefs. But what about me? If he's discovered here — despite what you say . . . And what about Gordon? If Gordon —" Mrs. Malherbe had sounded weary to the core; now she sounded fearful. "Oh, Robert!"

"I will leave." Tsumalo's deeper voice. "I will go. I do not mean to bring trouble to your house."

"No!" It was Robert. "It would be suicide. Ma, you don't realize. If they get him, they'll kill him. But not before they've tortured him. I can't put it clearer than that."

Mrs. Malherbe sighed and was silent. "Well, then, he can't go. Can he?" she said finally. "Mr. Ngenge, you may stay. But you must move into the house. It will be safer. We have a box room. It's hardly luxurious, but Mr. Malherbe has never set foot in it."

"There is a bed." Joshua could hear her push the chair back and get to her feet. "Robert will give you some sheets from the cupboard. Beauty can look after you." She laughed shortly. "I'm sure she does already. So my big grocery bill isn't just because the boy is growing so fast; it's because of our extra guest."

There were footsteps toward the door, and Joshua shrank back. "Robert, I am going to bed. Good night, Mr. Ngenge. Please excuse me."

"Good night, Madam. Thank you, Madam."

Joshua shut the door as quietly as he could and crouched

84

in the dark as Mrs. Malherbe went through the baize door, down the corridor, and slowly up the stairs.

As soon as he heard her door close, he ran lightly up to the spare room, the brass carpet rods cold beneath his toes.

Beauty stirred as he got back into the bed. He lay as still as he could, hardly breathing, thinking he would never sleep again.

Chapter Twenty

In the morning, the sky was clean and the clouds were high and bright. Puddles stood on the driveway, torn fig branches lay on the paving, and the pool was full of leaves.

Joshua stood, surveying the damage. Normally the pool was drained and covered in the winter; somehow, things had slipped this year. There were shutters that needed repairing; the upstairs veranda was leaking. The leaves should have been cleared away by now. The lawn, he saw, was long, and its edges weren't as neat as usual. Goodman had had trouble getting in to work. There were bad days and good days in the townships; when there were riots, the buses didn't run. And in any case, when the police were in Guguletu, Goodman didn't like to leave his wife and children on their own. When he did come, he was preoccupied. He stood talking with Beauty, drinking his tea at the kitchen door, the rake propped carelessly against the back steps just where Mrs. Malherbe might fall over it.

Joshua looked up at Table Mountain. Scraps of mist

hung over its flat edge in wisps: the tablecloth of cloud it was named for. The north wind must be blowing hard up there; its raw edges were rattling the hedges and whipping the curtains at Mrs. Malherbe's window.

He should get back inside. He would leave the pool for later. There were fewer frogs now that the weather was colder. He had released his little frog on the common one evening by the pond, hoping it wouldn't try to come back across the road and get squashed.

Then there was a sound in the road that he knew. The horn sounded loud in the morning air as Mr. Malherbe's car pulled up at the iron gates. He ran to open them.

He looked up and saw Mrs. Malherbe's face at the window, a white flash; then she was gone.

Joshua ran for cover.

The trouble didn't start straightaway. Mr. Malherbe was tired. He dumped his suitcase in the hall, took a shower, and went to bed. He had had difficulty getting home from the airport. There were armored personnel carriers on the road ("tanks," said Tsumalo), and a stone had clipped the Mercedes's silver wing.

No, it started later, when Mr. Malherbe woke for supper. Only it was eight o'clock already, and supper had been ready since seven.

Mrs. Malherbe and Robert had eaten; Robert had gone out.

Mr. Malherbe started by dumping his supper in the trash. Then he went rummaging in the fridge for bacon and eggs. Beauty was still washing up. She kept her head down and her hands in the sink.

"Why is there no beer?" he asked.

"I don't know, Master," she said, looking down and away. She knew the best thing was never to look at whites if you could help it. She had told Joshua this. Don't meet their eyes, she had said. They don't like it.

"I said, why is there no beer?" He stepped closer.

Beauty wasn't in charge of buying the beer or storing the beer, and she certainly never drank any of it. She didn't know what to do, so she kept washing up. She knew the beer had been drunk by Robert, and that he had given one or two to Tsumalo, but she had no intention of saying so.

The next thing she knew, Mr. Malherbe had ripped the washcloth out of her hand, spun her around, and was holding her chin up so she had to look at him.

"Look at me when I'm talking to you, damn you!" he shouted. "WHY—IS—THERE—NO—BEER?"

Beauty continued to avoid looking at him, afraid of what he might see in her eyes. And that might make him even angrier.

"The beers are finished, Master," she said finally. After all, no one had known he was coming home. He wasn't due back till Friday. Mrs. Malherbe would have gone shopping before then. In any case, they had all had their minds on other things. That was another thing she couldn't tell him.

"WHO—HAS—DRUNK—THEM, THEN?"

Beauty stood by the sink, her chin held in his firm grip. She looked relieved to see Mrs. Malherbe come in.

But this was a mistake too. Mr. Malherbe was not normally mollified by Mrs. Malherbe. If anything, she seemed to aggravate him.

"Gordon!" said Mrs. Malherbe. "What are you doing!" Uncharacteristically, she said, "Leave the washing up, Beauty, I'll do it later. You go to your room."

Mr. Malherbe let Beauty go. Neither Mr. nor Mrs. Malherbe knew that Joshua was in his hidey-hole, arms around Betsy's ample neck, face hidden in her fur. He had heard everything; he heard what followed.

It seemed that Mrs. Malherbe was in a difficult mood herself. This too was unusual. She was normally careful around her husband.

He could hear her frying bacon, and then breaking eggs into the pan. As they hissed in the fat, she raised her voice to be heard above the noise.

"So, was it a good trip?" She didn't sound very friendly.

Mr. Malherbe grunted. Silence.

"How's Charlene?"

A longer silence, then, "What on earth do you mean?"

"I just mean, how's Charlene?"

"What the *hell* do you mean?"

"I mean, is she well? Did you have a good trip? I mean, how's Charlene since you saw her last? I mean, did you enjoy staying with her—again—instead of at the hotel, where they have *never heard of you?*"

Somebody—Mrs. Malherbe?—put the pan down with a bang.

There was an odd silence, as if something was happening;

what, Joshua couldn't say. It was a kind of stifled silence, as if there was a struggle going on. Should he come out? But what could he do?

He stayed where he was. He held Betsy so hard that she squeaked, and then, horrified, let her go. He felt his nose prickle and the tears start. He was tingling all over. He could not bear it; to stay in here while the Master did whatever he was doing to her. To do nothing.

He remembered what Tsumalo had said to him: "You want me to fix him?" And then: "That's what they like to think. That we can't. Do. Anything."

He opened the door a crack. Still, he could see nothing. What if he crept out, edged around the dog's basket, and through the door into the dining room? From there he could — and the box room was just up the stairs —

The blood-thump of his heart banged in his ears. He could hear nothing else.

Then he was out, and the dining-room door opened smoothly, and as he squeezed into the hallway, he saw through the crack of the kitchen door that Mrs. Malherbe was bent back over the table. Mr. Malherbe had both hands around her throat. He was leaning his full weight upon her, and one of her hands hung limply over the table's edge.

He ran up the stairs two at a time. He hammered with his fists on Tsumalo's door. "It's me!" he shouted. "Open the door! It's Mrs. Malherbe!" One moment too many, and . . .

The door opened. "Kitchen!" he shouted, and pointed with a trembling hand.

Without a word, Tsumalo took the stairs, holding the

90

banisters and swinging his good leg down, with Joshua following.

In the kitchen, Tsumalo pulled Mr. Malherbe off his wife. Holding him by the neck of his shirt with one hand, he punched him hard, once, on the jaw. It was neatly done; Mr. Malherbe, who had not said a word, crumpled to the floor.

Mrs. Malherbe lay motionless on the table. Tsumalo felt the pulse beneath her jawbone and lowered her carefully to the floor. He put a folded apron under her head. "Get your mother to ring for an ambulance!" he shouted at Joshua.

Tsumalo was bent over Mrs. Malherbe. He had pulled her up into a kitchen chair. He was trying to wake her. Joshua stood helplessly by the door.

Beauty was kneeling by the unconscious Mr. Malherbe with a damp cloth in her hand. But she didn't seem to know what to do with it; or perhaps she was just nervous to touch him.

"Madam. Wake up, Madam!" Tsumalo felt for her pulse again. "Wake up!" Joshua watched anxiously.

No one had heard the front door open, but into this melee ran Robert. The call of a siren followed him in. He looked terrified. "Ma!" he shouted. *"What are you doing!"* he screamed at Tsumalo, who glanced at him briefly, then ignored him. Then Robert saw Mr. Malherbe on the floor and understood.

Tsumalo slapped Mrs. Malherbe's face lightly. He shook her, and just as he slapped her face again, two policemen arrived.

Things began to happen, slowly, as if they were all under water. Tsumalo looked up, frozen. Joshua shouted: "No! It was the Master!"

Robert turned to the constable, as if in slow motion, his hands out in a placatory gesture. His mouth was open; he was trying to speak.

The constable drew his revolver from its holster; Tsumalo dropped Mrs. Malherbe's hand and sprang to the counter-top. He smashed the window; the policeman fired. Tsumalo fell into the yard through the shattered window.

Beauty screamed; Joshua whimpered. Mrs. Malherbe began to stir in her chair.

Joshua ran out onto the veranda and into the yard. The lights were on. Tsumalo was curled like a fetus around the giant red fist of the wound in his stomach. He was choking; blood streamed from his mouth and arms.

Beauty ran to Tsumalo; she knelt and cradled his head. Joshua stood with his fists clenched. Beauty wept softly; the shattered glass glittered around them like a fall of frost. Tsumalo, unable ever to say another word, shuddered once — a great, breathy shudder — and was still, while the black constable watched from the back door, and Robert hovered beyond like a ghost.

Far off, Joshua heard a siren. Then Mr. Malherbe's voice inside the kitchen: "Thank you, officer. No, she's just badly shaken up. I think she should be checked over, though. You men arrived just in time."

Chapter Twenty-one

Joshua couldn't see anything. He couldn't really breathe. The blanket smelled of Betsy and it was covering him and he was in the footwell of a car. The rest of the car didn't smell good, either. Someone had left a banana skin under the seat; its floury odor filled his nostrils. He was hungry. The suspension was shot. Every time the car hit a bump, it hurt. "Ow!" he yelled once.

The murmur of voices from the front of the car became a long *"Sssssst!"* and a hand came down onto his shoulder and pressed firmly. A familiar voice said, "You must not say a word. They will find you."

"I need to wee."

"Wait until it is dark. Then we will stop."

Joshua lay in a miserable ball and tried to distract himself. He thought of the events of the previous evening. He squeezed his eyes shut, but tears leaked out anyway. Tsumalo was dead. And where was his mother?

Sobs began to shake his body. He was quaking. He rose up out of the back of the car and clutched at the men in the front. "I can't . . . I can't . . ." They glanced at each other.

"We had better stop," said a voice.

"*Aaai,*" said the driver disapprovingly, but he swung the car down a side road without another word, and then it got bumpy and they stopped.

"Here."

The man in the front passenger seat pulled him out of the car, stood him up, and said, not unkindly, "Look—it's not far now. Be quick and we'll go on."

"Where's my mother?" he called. "Where is she?"

The driver leaned across to him. Joshua saw that he was one of the men from the swimming pool, the one with a face like a fox's. His name was Sindiso, Tsumalo had told him.

"You are with us to keep you away from the police," he said gently. In the half-dark he could see that Sindiso was smiling. "You attacked one of them. Robert had to pull you off."

Then there were a few mouthfuls of water from a can, and he was back under the hairy blanket. He tried to make himself small, holding his knees, closing his eyes, and fashioning a little loop in its edge for his nose so he could breathe. He had almost stopped shivering.

Where were they?

Then suddenly it was morning. He must have slept. He pulled the corner of the blanket back. Sunlight.

The men in front sounded cheerful. They heard him stirring, and one of them said, "We are safe now."

The blanket was flung back, and Sindiso smiled at him. "Joshua, you can get up now. You can get up on the backseat. Look where we are!"

94

Joshua saw mountains above him and drew in his breath. He saw grass, cows, huts. Quickly, he wound down the window, kneeled up on the seat, leaned out, and drank in big gulps of air as if it were water.

Sindiso turned around to him and laughed. "Yes," he said. "This is the air of freedom. Breathe deep!" And he threw back his head and laughed again.

There was so much Joshua wanted to ask. He opened his mouth to speak.

But he wouldn't find out everything he wanted to know for a long, long time.

PART TWO
1976 – 78

Chapter Twenty-two

Joshua lies on his stomach in the dust under a thorn tree and throws pebbles at a stump. It is searingly hot. And he has nothing to do. Nothing! He broods, chin on cupped hands. He has not seen Sindiso since arriving a week ago. They hadn't stayed long in Mozambique, with its cows and its huts and its green mountains. Now they are in Angola, in a training camp for the soldiers, Sindiso has explained.

This camp is in a scrubby landscape, with thorn trees and dust as far as the eye can see. There is a house on a hill in the center of it: an old farmhouse. Joshua sleeps in a little room at the back, a storeroom with a high window next to the maid's room, where Mama Bongani lives.

She gives him *mielie-pap* in the mornings. As far as he can see, she is as busy as his mother used to be, looking after the men. She has to cook and clean and wash. She looks tired. When he tries to talk to her, she shoos him away gently, as if he were a persistent puppy.

This morning she asks him to help. "Here, take these, Joshua," she says. "They are too heavy for me." It is early in the camp, and she has done the daily wash. Joshua lifts the wet sheets from the tub and twists them to squeeze out the water. He pins them onto the clothesline, struggling not to dip the corners in the dirt.

She joins him. "Joshua," she says. "Do you miss your family?"

"Yes, Mama," says Joshua.

"This is no place for a boy like you," says Mama Bongani. "You should be with your mother. She needs you."

Joshua continues to lift and peg the heavy sheets. He hesitates. "Mama," he asks, "Mama, where are your children?"

She puts down the big basket in the dirt and looks at him and sighs. She has a *doek* on her head, like his mother, only hers is bright yellow, not white. "Joshua, my babies are all grown and gone. My sons have gone to fight. One of them is in prison. My daughter is a maid in Johannesburg. That is why I am here. There is no future for any of us until we are all free.

"That is why I know that your mother is missing you. Just because your babies are grown does not mean you do not miss them."

Joshua looks up at her; she is framed against the sunlight, and he cannot see her face. "I am sure my mother would be happy that I am here, helping you." He feels a sudden impulse to hug her. "I'll get the other sheets," he says.

In the distance, beyond a stand of trees, he can hear someone shouting and the men shouting back as they march. He is not allowed to come too close. It could be dangerous if they are shooting. They are also learning to use bombs, Sindiso has explained.

"When they are trained, they will be going back to South Africa to plant bombs in military places," he said. "When you leave here, Joshua, you are never to talk of what you have seen here. It would place us all in great danger."

"When can I learn to shoot?" he asked Sindiso, leaning back against a tree. He lined up an imaginary sight with his right hand holding the trigger close to his eye, and his left arm held out as straight as a gun.

Sindiso laughed. "No, you are too young, Joshua. We do not make child soldiers here. Your job is to do your schoolwork."

Now Joshua broods, alone under the tree. Trying to do his schoolwork on his own is hard.

He still thinks of it, the terrifying journey north, the searing air of Mozambique, the long, hot drive to this camp. He is assailed by a cramping grief whenever he has any time to himself. He wishes he could get a big rusty old key and turn back the clock. To see his mother and his little sister and brother. And to make Tsumalo and Sipho alive again.

He is so angry.

But for now he is helpless. And bored. He is the only boy in the camp. He rolls over onto his back and looks up through the thorn tree's scraggy, spiky branches at the relentless blue of the sky; it is almost too bright to look at. His eyes are watering, and he squeezes them shut. His clothes are covered in dust. Mama Bongani will be angry. It will make more work for her.

He opens his eyes, and a face swims into view between him and the sky. It is smiling. It is white. It's a girl's face. He sits up in surprise. He has not seen any white people here.

"Are you bored?" asks the face. It has sea-green eyes and long brown hair tied back in a ponytail. "Come with me." He jumps up and follows obediently. Her name is Bonny. She is from Jo'burg, she says. She is holding his hand like his mother used to do. Suddenly his eyes fill with tears. She glances down at him but says nothing.

"Listen," she says. Joshua sees a big man leaning forward. He is sitting on a tree trunk. The men gathered around him fall silent.

Joshua stands at the edge of the circle with Bonny. The big man has a big smile. He looks open and friendly. His audience is rapt; he holds them in the palm of his hand. He is telling a story about a herder boy. Then he looks up and sees Joshua. His broad face creases again into a smile, the eyes almost disappearing. "Come!" he commands.

"Go!" whispers Bonny, releasing him.

Joshua is nervous. But he is drawn and pushed forward by many hands until he stands by the man, in the crook of his arm.

"Now, do you see this boy? This boy is why we are fighting. And we are going to win. Are we going to win?"

"Amandla," comes the reply. *"Amandla."* Power.

Joshua feels uneasy. He can feel the heat coming off the man. And something else: it is the absolute, keen ambition of him, the intensity of his concentration on drawing those around him into his orbit. He wriggles free and pushes back into the crowd.

Bonny is waiting. She gives him a grin and holds out her hand.

"Who is he?" he asks.

"His name is Jacob," she says. "He used to be a herder boy himself. When the change comes, he will be in the government."

Chapter Twenty-three

With Bonny, he works an hour a day on his reading. She helps him to write a letter to his mother, carefully couched in vague terms. He is "enjoying his holiday," and he is "keeping up with his lessons." It won't be posted from here, Bonny says. It will be passed from hand to hand until it can be sent from Johannesburg.

"What about Tsumalo?" he asks. "What did he do? He wouldn't tell me."

"He was involved in the labor union movement," Bonny explains. "He was working to get workers the right to strike. They were making banners for a march when the police came. They can keep you in prison for a long time without putting you on trial. And on the night he escaped, he killed a guard."

Joshua feels a cold hand close around his throat. He looks at Bonny.

"He had to do it," she says. "They were torturing him."

"Yes," says Joshua. "But how did he get out?"

"One of the black prison guards helped him. He lent

him an old guard's uniform, and one afternoon when they were working in the grounds of the prison, he managed to slip away.

"Tsumalo hid in a tree, and when the guard walked under it, he jumped him and got the gun off him. When the others heard the shot, they thought it was Tsumalo who had been killed."

Joshua is silent. He doesn't like to think of Tsumalo killing someone. But he doesn't like to think of him being tortured either.

He picks up a stick and begins to scratch it in the sand. They are under the thorn tree, looking down on the camp.

No child is allowed to become a soldier; in this, the struggle is different to those in other countries, Bonny says. It is important for children to get an education — something they are denied under apartheid.

"When you are grown up, you can decide. Only then. Then you can join *Umkhonto we Sizwe*," says Bonny. It means "Spear of the Nation." He likes the words. They make him feel safe. These are the soldiers who are being trained in the camp and will go back to South Africa on bombing missions. They are the military wing of the African National Congress, which is fighting to overturn the apartheid government.

"What are you doing here, Bonny?" Joshua asks. He does not say "because you are a white girl," but that's what he means.

"Joshua, there are a lot of young people like me who believe in the struggle," she says. "Some of them stay in

South Africa, and some come out of the country to train," she explains.

She is twenty-one; she left as soon as she finished her degree at Rhodes University in the Eastern Cape. There were terrible forced removals to the area, she had told him. "People were dumped in the veld with nothing but a stand-pipe for water. They starved. Two out of three children died before they reached two years old, Joshua. Two out of every three!

"I knew then that I would have to leave," says Bonny. And she looks away. "How could I live in a country that could do that to its own people?

"If I stayed, I would be supporting the system just by being there. Now I have left, I can help bring it down." She is in the camp to train; she will go back soon and live underground until she is needed.

Joshua is astonished that white people are training too. "There is the world that everyone sees," explains Bonny. "That is the world of white privilege. Many white people think, *Why would we want to change that world?* But then there is also the world beneath that one, the secret place where we operate. And because we are white, there are places we can go and things we can do that are easier for us — much easier."

She gives Joshua a hug. "Things will change," she says. "It will take a long time, but it will happen."

And she tucks her shiny brown hair behind her ear and smiles at him — sadly, he thinks.

* * *

The next morning Bonny shakes him awake. It is early and still dark, and he is deep in a dream about home: he has his little sister and brother, one in each arm, and they are sitting outside his grandparents' house in the evening sunshine. "Come! Come now!" Bonny commands. He jumps out of bed, grabs his sweater, and runs.

They sit under a tree as the red sun rises slowly behind the black thorn trees and its cold beams find their shivering bodies. Bonny is crying.

"What is it? What is it?" he repeats.

"They've killed him," she says simply. "He's dead."

"Who's dead?" he asks.

"Steve Biko. He was the leader of the Black Consciousness Movement. He was a great man. He was arrested last month. He was tortured, Joshua. And they drove him a thousand kilometers to Pretoria with a terrible head wound — naked — chained in the back of a truck. And now he has died."

And she takes his hands in hers. "Murdered, Joshua."

"Like Sipho," he says.

"Yes," she answers gently. "Like Sipho."

Joshua can't get the thought out of his head. Chained like an animal in the back of a van, driven all those miles in terrible pain.

Bonny shows him a small picture torn from a newspaper. "Bantu Stephen Biko," says the caption. He has wide-set eyes and a level gaze. It's a handsome face.

The news has given Joshua a cold feeling in his stomach, a spreading feeling of dread that he wakes with every day and that reminds him of how he would wake every morning after the news of Sipho; with a nameless fear, but without remembering why. Only once he is fully awake does grief hit him with renewed force.

He says a prayer for his mother and his family, for Sipho and for Tsumalo, every night when he goes to bed. Now he adds Biko's name to his list.

And lying there in the dark, he swears to himself that when he grows up, he too will be a freedom fighter. He knows that there are thousands of men like Biko who have died at the hands of the police, men whose names he may never know. "It's too much. It's too much," he whispers to himself.

Chapter Twenty-four

Today Joshua is on his own. Bonny is away training for the day. She doesn't tell him why or where. It's a secret, she says. And he recalls how Tsumalo told him it was safer not to know too much.

Alone, he kicks around the camp with nothing to do. Bonny left him reading, but he is bored with it. He decides to go exploring. It's not allowed, but he doesn't care. He knows it's safer for him to stay in the main part of the camp.

He takes a quick look around—all the men are down at the range. The camp is almost empty, except for Mama Bongani hanging up the camp commandant's uniform on the line behind the house. He can see the bright yellow dot of her head scarf.

Away from the main buildings and the shooting range, right at the edge of the camp, just inside the barbed-wire fence and behind a stand of scrubby trees, there is a building that looks deserted. As he approaches, though, he can hear something. A small sound, a sound that's almost swallowed before it begins. Joshua is transfixed and stops, frozen, trying to hear it again. "Aaaah."

Was that it? It's almost whispered. He looks around him. It's quiet.

He turns his attention back to the building. It's the sound of someone in pain. He tiptoes closer. "Hello?" he whispers. Silence. Then another groan, louder, quickly stifled, as if whoever it is could not stop it emerging.

"Hello? Is there someone there? Are you OK?" As he says it, it sounds stupid.

Now he can hear a scratching noise. There is a vent at the top of the wall, the kind made by a brick with holes in it. That must be where the noise is coming from. As he watches, something drops out of it and lands at his feet. He scoots back in fright. It's a wad of paper, scrunched up small. Hardly daring, he picks it up gingerly and opens it out. On it there is a word, scratched in rough capitals with what looks like charcoal: "HELP."

Breathless, he runs around to the other side of the building. There is a stable door, firmly bolted, with a padlock. Why is there someone imprisoned here? The thought makes him go cold.

He looks around again. No one. Up to the door and "Hello!" he whispers. "Hello, who is there, please?"

A thin, dry whisper. "Help me, please. Help me." The voice fades away on the last syllables, as if the man inside can hardly speak, as if he is hardly there anymore.

"I can't—there is a padlock," Joshua whispers back urgently. "I'm sorry. Why are you locked up?"

A pause. It goes on so long that Joshua wonders if the man has fallen unconscious.

"They say I am a traitor." A creak rather than a whisper. Then another long pause. "But I am not. I am not."

Then a noise that is hard to interpret, a terrible noise that is like choking, but that Joshua realizes is the sound of crying.

Then another sound. But it comes over from the edge of the camp. He turns to run back toward his thorn tree, falling into a stroll as the Jeeps come into view, thrashing the grasses with a stick as if he is bored.

The knowledge that the man is there sits heavy with him; he watches as a Jeep goes across to the building and, later, back again. He is a spy under his tree on the hillock that overlooks the camp. There is an innocent man locked up in a stable. Is he to do nothing?

That night he and Bonny talk by the fire outside the tents. She puts an arm around him. "You're shivering, Josh." She has taken to calling him Josh, in the way that white people have of shortening everybody's names, no matter how short they are already.

He stiffens. "I'm fine." He does not want to tell her of his discovery. Yet he does. She is his only friend here. Who else can he tell? He can't do nothing. That would be wrong. He feels the knowledge sitting in his stomach like a weight.

Bonny swings him around to face her in the flickering light. "What's wrong? You were fine this morning."

"Nothing."

Soon they have retreated from the flames, and using the scant light of a penlight that Bonny fetches from her tent, they are approaching the stable.

It's apparent that there is some activity there. There is a Jeep parked outside it, light floods out from the door, and from inside the stable are coming terrible noises. Bonny turns and claps her hands over Joshua's ears. He wriggles free. He looks into her eyes in the half-light. And he can see that she knows what's happening.

"Come!" she commands. She drags and pushes and punches him away from the building until they are at the far side of the camp, away from everything: the house, the stable, the tents.

"What is it? What has he done? Why can't we help him?" The questions pour out of Joshua like lava in a stream she can't stem.

"We can't help him," she says simply. "I'm so sorry, Josh. There is nothing we can do."

And as he starts to protest: "No, I mean it." She emphasizes the words. "There—is—nothing—we—can—do. I'm so sorry." She pauses. "He is a spy sent by the police into the camp to find out our plans for the next attacks. He would have passed them back to the police. Then our men—our men, Josh—would have been picked off by the police like so many sitting ducks."

"But he says he is innocent," says Joshua. "Why would a black man spy for the police?"

"Of course he would say that, Josh. I'm sorry."

She gives him a hug, then pulls away, holding him by the arms and looking at him. He can only see her silhouette against the starlit sky. "It is difficult to find out that people are not always what they seem."

Josh thinks of the man's voice. Somehow he knows that he wasn't lying.

He looks up at Bonny and forces himself to relax his stiff shoulders. "OK. I understand. Let's go back before they miss us."

Joshua lies all night with his sleeping bag pulled up under his chin, drifting in and out of sleep, shivering. Does the man have a blanket? Is he hungry?

In the morning, he offers to wash up for Mama Bongani after they eat their *mielie-pap* at the kitchen table. As soon as she has left the house, he takes two slices off the loaf of rough bread and two thin slices of cheese. He wraps the sandwich in a bit of brown paper and stuffs it in his shorts pocket. It is not much, but it will have to do.

He wanders off to the thorn tree and lies there for a bit. Bonny, Sindiso, and some of the others are away training, and the camp is quiet. He considers taking the food to the man now, but it is only at the end of the day, when the red sun sinks over the far hill, that he feels safe enough. First, though, he fetches an old Coke bottle, fills it with water, and stuffs a rag in the top.

The dark is almost complete and wraps him like a secret. He approaches the stables using a zigzag route, almost out to the boundary and back, wandering quietly, head down, through the trees. Then he is below the blank brick wall with its vent.

"Hello," he whispers. "Are you there?"

There is a square gap in the bricks high up by the door of the stable, where one has fallen out. It is just big enough to slide the sandwich and the bottle through.

"Thank you," whispers the man inside.

Joshua sits huddled against the brick wall that has been warmed by the sun and waits, alert for any sound. Then he stands up and puts his mouth to the gap. "Give me back the paper and the bottle," he murmurs. "I will bring you more food tomorrow."

The next morning, he is heading out of the kitchen with a wrapped sandwich in his hand.

"Where are you going?" It is Mama Bongani, coming around the corner with an armful of laundry. He does not know what to say. She is looking at the sandwich. "What is that?"

He gives her an anxious smile. "I am sorry, Mama. I thought I would take something for my lunch." He has never done it before. It makes no sense. She will be suspicious.

She smiles at him. "That's a good idea. See you later."

He steps aside and she goes into the kitchen with the washing.

"Wait!" she calls. "Joshua, wait!"

He stands frozen. She comes out with a dripping Coke bottle, filled with water and corked.

"Thank you, Mama. Thank you." He smiles shyly at her, ducks his head, and runs.

On the third morning, he makes the sandwich and fills the bottle, but it isn't until dusk falls that he scrambles down the hill. But as he follows the path through the trees, he sees light filtering through the branches. The Jeep is outside, and there is light coming out of the doorway. He turns and runs: this time he can't listen. He kneels in the sand under the thorn tree, hands clenched together, and prays, and weeps. Then he stands up. He knows what he has to do.

He couldn't help Sipho, murdered hundreds of miles away from him, or Tsumalo, shot down right in front of him. But he can help this man. And he will.

It is the deepest, darkest time of the night. Joshua hasn't slept. He can't. He wriggles out of his sleeping bag and opens the door a crack. It creaks. This is the most dangerous part. Mama Bongani might hear him.

Out from under the bundle of clothes he uses as a pillow, he brings the flashlight. Bonny gave it to him the night he took her to the stable. "Have this," she said. "I have another one in my tent." She could see he was still upset. As if a flashlight would make him feel better!

He's never had a flashlight before. He doesn't plan to use it. He is going to give it to the man. And he has to take the bolt cutters he has seen in the lean-to by his room.

At the stable all is silent. The sliver of moon casts

the faintest of lights. Joshua listens at the door. Is it his imagination or can he hear breathing? Is the man asleep?

"*Sssst!*" Joshua hisses. "*Sssst!*"

Nothing.

"*Sssst!* Wake up!"

He doesn't want to cut the padlock until the man is awake. He rattles the door a bit and immediately hears a gasp from inside. "It's me!" he says quickly. Some instinct has prevented him from giving his name to the man or asking his. "I will let you out. I am going to cut the lock."

Silence. "Thank you," comes a hoarse whisper. "You are an angel."

Outside Joshua hesitates. He picks up the heavy cutters and weighs them in his hand. It isn't going to be easy.

"The key." The man's voice is still a whisper, but it is stronger now. "Look under the stone. I think they keep it there."

And there it is. Under a big stone by the door. It is the work of a moment to unlock it.

Inside, the man is sitting on the bare floor, slumped against the wall. His face is a mass of bruises; one eye is almost shut. He flinches from the light.

"Here." Joshua kneels by him and hands him the water. Half of it runs down his chin. Then he grabs the bottle and sucks at it desperately, half choking, gulping. "Slowly," commands Joshua. "You will get sick."

He leans back and takes a proper look. "Can you walk? Do you think you can make it across the river? If they catch you—"

"I will go," says the man, looking with his good eye into Joshua's face. "I would rather die than stay here."

Joshua's heart is thumping so loudly, he thinks the man will hear it. He helps him to his feet and to the door, grabbing a filthy blanket from the floor and wrapping it around him like a shawl. "Here," he says. "I have brought you some food. And more water. You will need that especially." He has put the bottle and the sandwich along with the flashlight in an old shopping bag. It isn't much, but it is the best he can do.

The two stand at the door and look into the darkness and listen. They can hear nothing but the high singsong of crickets and the faint rustles of the bush at night. No footsteps. Just the faint high glitter of the stars. It's good that the moon is not full.

"Ready?" asks Joshua.

"Yes," answers the man.

They begin their slow journey to the river. It is half a mile away. The man leans his heavy frame on Joshua. Beyond, the land is kinder, with more scrubby trees and paths through it, more cover for the day. It is two days' walk to the nearest farm. There he can say he is a refugee. If he is lucky, he will meet with kindness before he resumes his journey. The farther away he gets, the more likely it will be that no one will be able to identify him and the more likely it will be that he will survive.

They are silent as they walk along the sandy path through the scrubby bushes. As they come out in sight of the river, the man sags against him suddenly. He is breathing heavily. "Not far now," says Joshua.

The river is not deep at this point. It's only waist high, but there are strong currents, and Joshua is worried the man won't have the strength to get across. He helps him to tie the bag around his neck to keep it out of the water. He has no shoes.

The man takes Joshua's hands in his big ones and looks hard at him. "What is your name?"

Joshua hesitates. It is not good to share information, he knows that. Nevertheless . . . "Joshua," he answers.

The man takes a sharp breath, as if he has felt a sudden pain in his chest. "A long time ago, I had a son called Joshua," he says softly. And he turns his face away. Joshua's heart leaps. Perhaps — "He's dead now," says the man, and turns a bleak face to him.

"Go," says Joshua, and pushes him gently toward the river.

"Aaaah," says the man as he wades into the cold water. He turns to Joshua. "I will never forget you." The faint moon gleams on his upturned face; the one good eye glitters. Then he is gone, holding the bag firmly across his chest with folded arms and carefully feeling his way with his feet, swaying as the force of the water hits him.

Joshua watches him anxiously. In a minute he is across safely. He scrambles up the bank, stands, and turns to wave. Then the bush swallows him, and it is as if he has never been.

Joshua takes a deep breath where he has been crouching. Then there is a touch on his shoulder, and he whips around in terror.

"You fool," says Bonny. He can barely see her face, but he can hear her fury. "You were stupid to believe him," she says. "He was lying to you."

Joshua does not speak of the ridiculous hope that sprang up in his chest when the man said: "Once I had a son called Joshua."

She looks closely at him in the moonlight. "Come on," she says. "No time to lose. If they see us out here, they will know what you've done."

Wordlessly they run back to the stable and lock it up again, and he shows her where to put the key back under the stone.

Then they part company, Joshua to put the bolt cutters back where he found them and to jump back into bed, and Bonny, tight-lipped, to her tent. As he lies in the dark, unable to sleep, Joshua recalls how she said: "They will know what you've done."

Chapter Twenty-five

I t is early morning; the sliver of moon is still visible in the pale sky. There is a flurry of activity as a Jeep speeds back to the house from the stable in a plume of dust. Joshua lies with his book under his thorn tree, watching without appearing to watch, as the commander comes out of the house. He can see the men gesticulating and pointing. They all go back to the stable.

Then they drive in the direction of the river. Two men get out and wade across. They disappear into the bush. Joshua watches them go with a feeling of dread. Will they catch up with the man, sick and injured as he is? With a cold feeling, he recalls the flashlight that he gave him — Bonny's flashlight.

But the men come back on their own.

He goes to find Bonny. "Why haven't they questioned everybody? They must realize that someone here let him out."

She doesn't look at him. "He was a secret. That was the point, Joshua. No one was allowed to know he was here. Now they can't admit that he ever was."

* * *

Afternoon; he is lying again under his tree staring at the cerulean sky, praying that the prisoner got away. Could he have gotten far enough away by daylight? Could he have found someone to help him?

Soon his question is answered. Through the farthest gate comes a cloud of dust that grows bigger and, as it approaches, turns into a Jeep. It skids to a halt outside the house, and two men run inside. They come out with the commander.

It all happens very quickly. The back door of the Jeep is pulled roughly open, and the men pull someone out. Even from this distance, Joshua can see it is the prisoner. They are hitting him. Joshua cannot look at the stick figures in the distance that are doing these awful things. He lies flat in the dust on his stomach, with his hands over his ears and his eyes shut, as he did when he was younger, as if this would prevent them from seeing him as well as him from seeing them.

Tears stream down his cheeks into the dust. He is sobbing out loud. And there is a tiny kernel of fear there too. Will the man give him away? Can he lie here and just let this happen?

Then he jumps to his feet and runs down the hill as fast as he can. He skids to a halt right by the men, and they turn in surprise.

A silence. Into the middle of it he says: "It was me. I let him go."

The shock is palpable. The men look to the commandant. They start toward Joshua. "No," he says, and stills them with

121

a hand gesture. The prisoner, whose mouth is bleeding, looks away.

Joshua finds that now he has said this, he can say no more. The commandant turns to the prisoner.

"I didn't see who freed me," he says, his face stony, his eyes fixed on the ground. "Someone just unlocked the door. It was open when I pushed against it."

"It was me," says Joshua again. The silence deepens and widens. Then, somehow, terribly, he has mentioned Bonny. "Bonny found out and she was angry with me."

Then there is a voice behind him. A deep voice, a gentle voice, a commanding voice; a voice he knows. "It was me. I let him go." It is Sindiso.

The prisoner draws a breath in suddenly. But he says nothing. Joshua knows what that breath means. How can he say it wasn't Sindiso when he has just said that he didn't see who it was?

The men grab Sindiso and twist his arms up behind his back. "Leave him," says the commandant. It is clear to him that Sindiso is protecting the boy. And yet—

"I gave him Bonny's flashlight—the one she gave me." This time Joshua's voice is stronger. Sindiso stares bleakly at him. *Don't,* says the look. *Don't go on and especially don't talk about Bonny.*

But he can't stop. "Did you find it?"

Silently, one of the men pulls a flashlight out from his pocket. It looks so tiny, barely big enough to take two penlight batteries. It is bright orange and looks incongruous lying across the man's broad palm.

"It was the girl," says the commandant. "We should never have trusted her. She is a spy. Of course. We were stupid not to see it."

"No!" says Joshua. "It was me. Bonny told me not to do it!"

Somehow, impossibly, this makes it sound worse.

Joshua casts a desperate look at the prisoner.

Please, say his eyes. *Please tell them it was me, or they will think it was Bonny.*

He feels as if he is struggling underwater. He can't get them to hear or understand.

"Look," he says, turning toward them all, his hands out as if to stop them thinking the wrong thing, doing the wrong thing.

"It was me." He stops and draws his slight body up to his full height. "I went by the stable and heard a voice. He asked me for help"—he gestures toward the prisoner without really looking at him. "And I couldn't bear to just leave him there. Not after what happened to Tsumalo. And my brother Sipho. And now Steve Biko!"

He pauses and takes a breath. "I told Bonny. She told me he was a traitor. She told me how he planned to betray us. She thought I understood."

Another pause. Now he finds he can't look at the man.

"I didn't believe her. I let him out. I led him . . ." and his voice falters. "I led him to the river, and I watched him cross it, and then . . . then . . ." His voice begins to break. "Bonny appeared. She had followed me. She was furious with me. You mustn't think it was her. She understands that this man is a traitor. But I don't."

And he goes up to the commandant and stands before him. The men move toward Joshua, but again the commandant shakes his head.

"If we believe it is not right for the government to torture us, how is it right for us to torture this man, whether or not he is a traitor?" Joshua can't believe he is saying these things.

He is dizzy; he sways slightly on his feet. But he is still full of what he wants to say.

"If we kill him, we are no better than them." There is contempt in his voice. "We don't even know if he is a traitor."

He is aware of the eyes of the commandant, which are locked on his. The man opens his mouth to speak.

But now there is a noise in his head, which seems to grow and grow and fill every space in it.

"Look out!" shouts Sindiso.

The sky is full, incredibly, of sound, and something hits him hard and throws him to the ground.

There is screaming and crying.

Then silence.

Joshua can't move his limbs. He can't breathe. He is pinned to the ground by something heavy. He opens his eyes and finds that someone is lying on top of him. It is the prisoner.

He wriggles himself free, but the man is still unconscious. Sindiso is crouching by him.

"Joshua, come."

"But —"

Sindiso touches his shoulder briefly.

Joshua looks at the man, lying sprawled where he had thrown himself on Joshua as the planes came over and the bombs began to fall. His eyes are closed, his face relaxed as if in sleep.

Sindiso crouches by him and touches his fingers to the man's wrist. He shakes his head. Joshua understands. "We must go."

Joshua gets to his feet slowly, painfully, as if he is an old man. He looks around him.

Where the house was, there is a hole in the ground surrounded by rubble.

He can't see Mama Bongani.

Farther away, the stables are gone. A pall of smoke hangs low over the camp.

Around him there is only silence.

PART THREE
1978

Chapter Twenty-six

It has been a long journey, but now they are close to Cape Town. Their lift drops them near the cooling towers, and they walk a little way back up a dirt path to the national road, away from the rotten-egg stink. "Wait here," says Sindiso. "I'll call you when someone stops." He smiles at Joshua. "Not far now."

He steps out from the scrub to the edge of the road. It is Joshua's turn to carry the rucksack with its heavy load, and he is tired. He sits down behind a wattle bush and stretches his legs out, leaning into the springy, dusty branches and closing his eyes.

There is a squeal of brakes and the whir of a car backing up. Joshua, startled out of a half-doze, begins to scramble to his feet. But there is an odd silence, and instead of stepping out onto the road, he crouches down and holds his breath. He can see three pairs of feet through the gaps at the bottom of the foliage, staggering from left to right and back again.

Sindiso grunts with each blow. Joshua squints through the branches. He thinks that he sees a frantic eye for a moment—Sindiso's? Then the men push him into the car and are gone. He sits down abruptly on the dusty ground. The straps of the rucksack dig into his shoulders.

Police? They must have been. Quietly, Joshua wraps his arms around his folded legs and rocks, desperately trying to quell the swelling anxiety in his stomach. He will not cry. He will not. He is grown up now. The time for crying is past. But he is racked with pain. Sindiso too? Not Sindiso. Where have they taken him? What will they do to him? He closes his eyes and remembers Sipho. Tsumalo. Steve Biko, fatally injured, driven naked through the night.

After what seems a very long time, he gets up, hefts the rucksack, and continues along the national road behind a screen of oleander bushes with their vivid red poisonous flowers. After he thinks enough time has passed, he steps cautiously out onto the road and sticks out his thumb.

Joshua jumps down from the truck. "Hey, thanks, man." He smiles up at the driver. He slings his rucksack from one shoulder to the other. It's heavy and no wonder; he's carrying the limpet mines. He flexes the muscles in his shoulders. He was such a skinny kid. But he's two years older now.

And the place: here is the road he had run down. It is narrower, dingier. The leaves on the oak trees — he looks up, expecting to see feet pedaling and a Cheshire cat smile — the leaves look rusty.

He thinks of Sindiso. Where do they have him? He remembers the sounds that came from the stable in the camp. Then he pushes them away. There's no time to think of that now. Because he's alone, he'll have to move fast. There is more trouble. There are tanks in the townships again, the driver told him. He's in a white area, and if he's stopped, he won't have a pass. In spite of his new height, he still looks too young to be a laborer.

In five minutes he is there, ringing the bell in the high wall. The house is no more than a few streets away from Bonair Road, where he grew up. "I'm looking for work. I've just arrived from the Transkei." This is what they've agreed. This is a safe house, and the white couple here are expecting him — him and Sindiso.

A maid comes to open the wrought-iron gate. He repeats his lines to her — he has no idea whether she knows who he is, although her resentful look would suggest not. They walk in tandem down the brick path between neat rows of blue hydrangeas — named *Krismisblomme* for the time of year, the high summer of December. He shifts his burden again from one aching shoulder to the other; it's been a long journey.

The Madam and the Master are in a wood-paneled room. They have the blinds drawn, and slatted sunlight lies across the dim carpet. He blinks. "Hello." No, here that sounds wrong. He is not going to say, "Morning, Master; morning, Madam," as he would have done before. But he is aware that he is standing almost at attention.

Now he's used to not being black. Or, more accurately, used to not being subservient. This is what exile has done for him. Nevertheless, he ducks his head shyly.

"Please sit down," says the woman, smiling. He is offered

something to drink. They are having black tea in bone-china cups. He asks for a Coke.

He perches on a low wing chair and finds he is transfixed by the sight of two massive stuffed fish in glass cases, high on the wall.

He drags his attention to the couple, who, he finds, are both smiling at him, with kindness and a slight edge of amusement.

"My son and I caught those," says the man. He looks down. "He lives abroad now. So they remind me of him. Happier times"—and he looks up, directly at Joshua, who catches his breath. He can feel the man's sorrow from here. And instantly he thinks not of his own father, but of his friend Sindiso. Tears spring to his eyes. Stupid!

He explains what happened to Sindiso. "What a terrible, terrible thing. And you so young," says Mrs. Brown. She looks at him sympathetically. "So young and so brave." He shakes his head fiercely. He will not cry. But if he shuts his eyes, he can still see it.

Joshua opens his eyes. The Browns are looking at him. They expect him to say something. He shrugs. "I am all right," he says.

He hesitates. "There is one thing. I still have the limpet mines."

Chapter Twenty-seven

How strange, thinks Joshua, that he is staying in the house on the corner that he used to run past in fear of the two Dobermans. They are both dead, gone to chase black people in dog heaven, perhaps. The wrought-iron gates stand shut all the time now, and the new couple have a boxer and a Rhodesian ridgeback. Thankfully, once they are introduced to him, they leave him alone; he is inside the magic circle.

He is to stay in the gardener's hut; there is no gardener anymore. It's more comfortable than the one Tsumalo had used. There is a proper bed and an electric light. And he is welcome to use the inside bathroom; he doesn't have to share a bath with the dogs. He wonders whether Mandisa, their maid, knows about Mr. and Mrs. Brown's political affiliations. It's not discussed; she brings his meals with a slight pursing of the lips and doesn't offer any conversation.

During the day he sits quietly outside the hut on the camp chair they've provided. They lend him a book of poems by exiled poets. It's banned; their son sent it. Inside it he finds the lines:

All our land is scarred with terror,
rendered unlovely and unlovable;
sundered are we and all our passionate surrender,
but somehow tenderness survives.

Does it? he thinks. *Does tenderness survive?* He thinks of the couple in the house, alone, with their son in America. They had decided to stay. They knew the cost. They could be picked up any day. He wonders about Mandisa. He's noticed that unlike Mrs. Malherbe, they use her Xhosa name and not an English name. She seems hostile. But it's hard to tell. Perhaps she is just being careful. He puts his head back and closes his eyes against the sun, then reads on:

I am *the exile*
am the wanderer
the troubadour
(whatever they say)

gentle I am, and calm
and with abstracted pace
absorbed in planning,
courteous to servility

but wailings fill the chambers of my heart
and in my head
behind my quiet eyes
I hear the cries and sirens.

He closes the book. Again he feels the unbearable closeness of number 23. He has walked past it, in the early morning before anyone is up. Who lives there now?

Mr. Malherbe had stayed on, he had heard in the camp. He imagines him, more and more bitter, sitting by the pool, swilling that brandy muck he drank. One day the new maid came in and found him dead. His throat had been cut as he lay in his bed. There had been no dog to raise the alarm; not even a useless basset hound. Nothing had been taken. Not a thing. Not a bottle of whiskey from the bar, none of the silver. Nothing. The side door on the downstairs veranda was standing open, its glass smashed where they had gotten in.

When all is told, he cannot believe that the man who killed Mr. Malherbe would need to account for himself, was doing any more than setting the weights a little straighter in the scales of justice.

As he plans to do himself. He is going to set a limpet mine in the shopping center where Sindiso had planned to do it. Although he does not want to do it.

There is still no news of Sindiso. He imagines him there, sitting on the low stone wall by the shed, with his legs stretched out in front of him in the evening sun. His eyes are locked on Joshua's, and his gaze is severe.

"You must remember, Joshua," Sindiso had said, "that this bomb will be very important for us. It will say that even the white areas, the areas where white people go shopping and meet for coffee, the very places they think are the safest, are not safe. There is nowhere that is safe. We don't want to kill anyone. The shops will be closed. But the message will be strong."

Joshua wants to argue. What about the night watchman? What about passersby, coming home from the bioscope — the cinema? He tries to answer but can't; then he wakes, stiff in the canvas chair, his mouth dry. The sun has gone behind the plane trees and he is cold.

The Browns have told him that they would take him there in the station wagon. He would need to lie down in the back, they said, with the rucksack. They would take him near to the place, a turnout on the national road, and leave him there. That would be the safest thing.

He knows the city. He will get back on his own, hitch-hiking like last time. It will be harder without Sindiso. They had looked like a father and son, he'd thought. People were more likely to stop for them and less likely to be suspicious.

Joshua catches sight of himself in the scratched mirror on the shed wall. His eyes look a little wild. His face has broadened, the chin has gained definition, but it's still a narrow face, an anxious face, he thinks, a face that already bears the marks of his life. He closes his eyes and takes three deep breaths. Is this the right thing to do? It is designed to frighten, not to kill. But still . . .

Then he thinks again of Sipho. Tsumalo. Biko. And now Sindiso. And his shoulders straighten. He stands tall. He opens his eyes and stares into the mirror again. He is a man now. He will avenge them all.

Chapter Twenty-eight

A hand on his shoulder. "Time to get up." It's Mr. Brown.

Joshua is awake instantly. He has slept with the rucksack beside him. He's dressed beneath the sheet. "I am ready," he says, and jumps up.

He doesn't feel ready. There is a dream that is disappearing, though he wants to hold on to it: he is in a big crowd in a city square, and above him on a balcony there is a man. The cheering stops and the man begins to speak— *"It is an ideal for which I am prepared to die."*

Then—no, it's gone. All that remains is the roar of the crowd and the elation that had flooded through his body. Where was it? Who was it? There is a name they were chanting over and over: *Mandela. Mandela.*

"Nelson Mandela!" he says to himself. "Of course!" But he is in prison, on an island five miles out in Table Bay.

There's no time to think of this now. He bends awkwardly and pulls up the sheet. "Don't worry about it; please, Joshua, we'll do it."

In the back of the station wagon is a blanket. It is navy blue, soft, and smells of Omo washing powder. He climbs beneath it, stowing the rucksack behind the front seat. It will be OK. Limpet mines are quite stable, Sindiso said.

Mr. Brown gives him a wristwatch. It has a scratched face and a worn chestnut leather strap. "You'll need this," he says. Mrs. Brown smiles at him from the front seat.

She has a kind face, with a faint tracery of lines across it that appear when she smiles, which she does a lot; pale blue-gray eyes and faded blond hair. What if he killed someone like her?

He feels sick and dizzy. He smiles wanly at her, pulls the blanket over his head, and closes his eyes.

On the way into the shopping center, he walks by a group of children. They must be on a nursery school outing. They are crowded around their teacher, shouting and calling. He keeps his head down. He has his overalls on and a cap pulled low, a disguise he hopes renders him invisible.

He glances at them just once and catches the gaze of a blue-eyed boy with straight white-blond hair. The child frowns at him for a moment, as if he recognizes him, then turns away and places his hand in the hand of his teacher. As they pass out of sight, he turns again and looks directly at Joshua.

It is only a glimpse, but it stays with him.

A limpet mine is an awkward, heavy thing. He is in a toilet cubicle, a tight fit even without a rucksack that has two of the metal spheres packed into it. He almost wishes

that someone had stopped him. Then he wouldn't be climbing onto the toilet seat and fishing around behind the high
old-fashioned cistern for a spot to attach it by its two big
magnets.

As he struggles to fix the heavy thing in place, he
struggles to remember where he has seen that steady gaze
before. Of course. Robert. The boy looked like Robert.

Joshua shakes his head, clearing his vision.

He stops dead, leaning on the wall, the mine cold and
metallic against his hands where he is holding it against
the cistern. For a swift moment, he is a small boy too, in
the dust of his own backyard, floating paper boats in the
little stream of water he had made by the tap, his mother in
the kitchen, Goodman edging the lawn. This whole world,
this difficult, dangerous, cruel world, is waiting for him —
waiting to pounce like a leopard from a tree in the veld on
the tiny, big-eyed *duiker* that tiptoes by on its delicate legs.

He can still hear the explosion of the policeman's gun
and see Tsumalo being shot and falling, being shot and
falling, again and again. The shower of glass, the opening
flower of blood, the spreading red on his mother's white
apron.

But he can see, too, the dust of the camp, the bowed
head of the prisoner, the commandant's eyes locked on his,
and he can hear his own words: "If we kill him, we are no
better than them."

And he sees again the sky-blue eyes of the boy, fixed
on his.

No. He can't do it.

He climbs down, wrestles the heavy thing off the cistern and back into his rucksack, and leaves the stall. As luck would have it, he sees a mop standing in a bucket of dirty water, catches it up, and begins wiping the floor with it just as a white man comes in, glances incuriously at him, and goes to the urinals on the end wall.

Joshua ducks his head in the direction of the man's back and walks out carrying the bucket and mop, which he leaves at the end of the hallway. He doesn't want to be accused of stealing anything. Not even a bucket of dirty water.

He leaves the shopping center behind him. He is dizzy and sick; he trips over a paving stone, losing his footing for a moment, and draws a sharp look from a sour-faced white woman passing by.

On the national road, he doesn't have long to wait. A cream Mercedes stops for him, one of the really old ones with tan leather seats whose diesel engines go *tick-tick-tick*. "Where to?" asks the driver. He's elderly, English-sounding, trim, upright, wearing his seat belt fastened tight across his white shirt and maroon tie. A navy blazer with a badge on the pocket is hanging up behind him.

"Rondebosch Common," mutters Joshua. "Please." He sits with his hands clenched between his knees to stop them shaking.

They drive in silence. The man pulls over into the bus stop. "So. Here we are, then," he says. He looks curiously at Joshua, who is leaning back against the seat with his eyes closed. "This is where you need to get out." Joshua opens his eyes. The man looks concerned. "Are you OK? You don't look well." It's six o'clock, still light.

Joshua gathers all his strength and smiles at him. It would have been far better to take a bus back, to be lost in the crowd. This man will remember dropping him in a white suburb; an act suspicious in itself for a young black man. He climbs out, hefts the rucksack, and leans back in. "No, I'm fine, Master, thank you. I've got to get my bus back to Jo'burg. It's coming soon."

He hopes that will put the man off his scent, so he won't think he's staying somewhere nearby, creeping in the back gate to borrow a bit of floor in the maid's room of one of the big houses.

"Thanks, Master." He feels absurdly grateful.

He shuts the heavy door, turns to wave, and heads in the direction he said he was going. Once the car has disappeared, he turns right at the traffic lights off the freeway, down Links Road, and right into Bonair, slipping through the gate of the house on the corner. The dogs rush up to him, jump up at him, pleased, wagging their tails — though the boxer only has a ridiculous little stump — and he strokes their heads. His hand is still shaking.

He sits down in the camp chair, his face in the last of the sun, then abruptly changes his mind and goes inside.

He lies curled up on the bed, eyes closed, hands tight between his thighs.

Chapter Twenty-nine

It is morning; light is pushing between the rough slats that make up the door. Joshua has slept. He checks the watch: five a.m.

He goes down the path on tiptoe, the concrete slabs cold under his feet, his shoes in his hand. Habit. The dogs come whispering out, wagging their whole bodies, rubbing against his legs, smiling up at him, if dogs could smile.

Now he is out in the road. And in a few minutes he is outside number 23, with its weeping willow and the loquat tree with its shiny dark leaves. The small yellow spheres hang from the branches. He can taste them instantly, their tartness, and up he goes. It is not so easy to hide now that he is bigger, and not quite so easy to climb: he has to struggle to lift himself by his arms, and then he is level with the bay window. He shivers. It was the window to the Malherbes' bedroom.

From the tree he can see down the side of the house; the riot of nasturtiums are still there, the tangle of orange and red and yellow, their lily-pad leaves hiding the ground. On the other side of the fence is the lawn of next door's house. It is as smooth as it had been; the house looks still and empty, although there is a car in the drive, a little red Mini. He hugs himself and shudders. He feels exposed. There aren't enough leaves around him. He is too big. What if someone looks out of the top window?

He gazes at it. Then a sound catches his attention, and he looks at the house next door. A light has come on inside. For a few moments nothing else happens. Then the heavy oak door opens, and out comes a young woman with a camera bag in her hand. Behind her there is a tall young man. He is carrying an overnight case. He stows the case in the tiny trunk. He takes the camera bag and puts it on the passenger seat. "Hey, sis." He holds out his hands and takes hers. "They're going to be angry. *Jislaaik,* man, are you sure you should go?"

She is tall and narrow, with a fall of brown hair to her shoulders.

"Stefan, I've got to go. I can't stay and listen to them go on and on. Especially when they say we are well rid of Biko. They drive me mad."

Joshua is alert, up in his tree.

"Come." The young man opens his arms wide, and she folds herself into them, her head on his shoulder, eyes shut. Then she straightens and pulls away.

"Can you get the gate?"

"Sure. You take care now, hey. And phone when you get there. Don't worry about me. I'll take the flak." He smiles down at her. His hair is blond, with tight curls, his face open and sunny.

143

Out of the open door hurtles a small figure; she throws herself at the young woman, and the two hug, the two dark heads close, the older girl laughing.

"I'll come back, Anna. Don't worry."

"Lizzie, don't go!" comes the querulous tone, and up in the tree Joshua smiles in recognition.

"I've got to. But I'll be back soon, I promise."

Stefan waits, and when the two have said good-bye, he lopes off down the drive and carefully lifts the iron gates across the drive so that they don't drag on the tarmac. He mock salutes as the little red car comes by, then closes the gates, but not before watching the Mini creep off up the road, its engine surprisingly loud in the early morning quiet.

He walks back up the drive, pausing to pull the disconsolate girl to his side. The liveliness has gone from him.

Joshua finds he has been holding the branch so hard that when he lifts his palm away, it holds the imprint of the bark. He swings himself down from the tree in a sudden motion, finding he does not care whether he is seen or not.

And so it is that as he passes the big wrought-iron gates and glances up the drive, he sees a small, sturdy woman coming down it, in the light blue uniform and the white apron and the *doek* that signifies the job of maid, and his heart painfully turns over in his chest. It is his mother. He knows it with a certainty that leaves him dizzy.

But as he leans a hand against the pillar, she looks up and he sees (of course!) that it is not. How can it be? She is in the Ciskei with his brother and sister, home at last with her family. He has not seen her since Sindiso grabbed him and pulled him out of these gates, her arms twisted brutally behind her by the white policeman, her cries ringing in his ears.

This woman has a light brown face and the bits of hair that escape from underneath the white scarf have a reddish tinge. Not Xhosa then. She is Colored. And about sixty, by the look of her—much older than his mother. She gives him a wide grin, a mischievous smile that envelops her whole face in a sea of wrinkles.

"Hey, what you doing here?" she asks. "This is *mos* a white area, you know." But her intonation is light, her tone jokey, and the word "white" she draws out, so that it seems to have several syllables rather than just one, like this: *"whyyyyyyutt."*

He is mute. But while she waits, her smile turning to a look of concern, he begins to recover his ability to speak. "I lived here," he manages to say, while she approaches and begins to rummage about in a mailbox attached to the gate.

It is her turn to be silent, and she regards him for several seconds before her puzzled look clears. Her eyes widen. "You!" she declares, and before he can demur, she has opened the side gate and pulled him through it. *"Kom!"* she commands.

Before he has time to think, he is following her back down the familiar drive and around into the yard, and then—horror, no, he can't do it—up the back *stoep* stairs and into the kitchen. There is the green door with its worn baize and dull brass studs, and the little door to the cupboard under the stairs, a low door that now seems barely big enough for a *tokolosh* to fit through.

"No," he tries to say. But there he is, inside, seated at the table, a different table, he notes, made not of speckled white iron but of shiny dark wood, and the woman is fussing with the kettle.

He is nervous about sitting here in this kitchen, even though now his legs can only just fit under the table. But she tells him that the owners are away on holiday in Durban. She is in charge. There is a golden Labrador called Temba, who runs in from the garden and lays his trusting head on the boy's lap and trembles and wags his tail, his brown eyes fixed on Joshua's.

Her name is Margie, she says, and she tells him about the Andersons. The father is a lawyer, the mother a GP. The two daughters have gone to live in England. She tells him to come back tonight and she will make him her special crumbed stockfish and her twice-fried chips.

But it is still early; by seven a.m. he is back in the garden shed down the road, in time to be called for breakfast.

Chapter Thirty

It is evening. "We all thought you were dead," says Margie. Her hair is still under the *doek,* but more of it has escaped now, and beads of sweat sit on her forehead as the oil seethes in the pan. She used to work up the road for the old Kloppers. Then, when Mr. Klopper died and Mrs. Klopper went into a home, she came to work here, at number 23.

"But—"

"Yes," she says. "I worked for Mr. Malherbe. I needed work, and I knew what that man was like, but I wasn't scared. Oh, no!" And she throws her head back and laughs. "He gave me no-o-o-o-o trouble."

Joshua finds this hard to believe, but decides to listen and not argue.

In any case, he knows she didn't have to work for him for long. "Lucky I was away or it would be me sitting in *tjoek,*" she says. "But the people who did it were so-o-o-o clever. They must have worn gloves. There were no fingerprints. And they stole nothing. Not a thing. The side door was unlocked."

"But—" said Joshua, thoughts forming fast. "But didn't the police think it was you who'd left the door unlocked?"

Margie turns from the stove. "That's why I broke the window before I called them." She smiles at him, but this time the smile does not reach her eyes. *I hated him too,* those eyes say. *We all did.*

She turns back to flip the fish in the pan. A faint smell of burned crumb reaches him. "It's quite easy. You just wrap your hand in a dishcloth." He realizes she is referring to breaking the window.

The fish is delicious, its white flakes soft under the crust of crumb. It tastes of the sea, or how he imagines the sea might taste. She has given him a small glass of beer to go with it; they are sharing a can. As she takes it out of the fridge, she catches his eye and shrugs. A small smile tugs at the edge of her thin mouth.

He thinks he likes her.

It is only after the meal, after he has told his story, gazing at the window where he had last seen Tsumalo alive, crouching like a lion, after he has fiercely dabbed a stubborn tear that escaped his eye, that she hesitates and says, "You know Tsumalo escaped."

"No." The word barely forms on lips that are suddenly dry. "No. He couldn't have. He was dead. I saw him." If only—if only—if only—"He was dead. He is dead." Now he really is crying, dashing the tears off his cheeks with the backs of his hands, bent over with a pain in his stomach so sharp that he thinks he might get sick.

She smiles at him, a real one this time, a real grin. "No. He was taken to the hospital. But the doctor who was doing the death certificate found a pulse. He didn't tell the police or they would have taken him away." She pauses for effect. "And *pouf*!"—she waves her hand as if it were a magic wand—"they made him disappear. First into intensive care, and then into the black men's ward, under another name. Then, once the bullets were out, his stomach wound healed—and it took a while—he was smuggled north, across the border."

Joshua found hope was forming despite himself. "Where is he now?" He wants to believe this story. Desperately.

"Nobody knows." Margie's air of triumph abates. "He was supposed to go to one of the training camps like the one you were in. But nobody knows where he went. He didn't get there."

And Joshua is forming another question, shaping it with his hands, when there is a little noise at the front of the house, beyond the baize door. Then, much louder, the high, sudden voice of a siren.

The Labrador erupts from the floor, barking wildly.

"Quick!" Margie hisses. "Out the window!" And as he hesitates: "*Polies! Gaan! Go!*"

Now he is out in the yard, landing with a thump, clumsily, on his knees in the yellow dirt, and running for the side of the house, crushing the nasturtiums beneath his feet, breathing hard. It is all but dark here; the sun has set, and there is barely room for him between the tall wooden fence that borders Anna's garden and the house walls beneath the high bay windows.

He is crouching, inhaling the sweet-sour smell of the squashed flowers, his hands over his ears, as if that would help. He can hear they are in the kitchen, crashing about, shouting at Margie. He can hear a police dog snarling and barking and thinks briefly of the mild-mannered Labrador.

At the end of the alleyway, he sees the loquat tree, scales it, and drops into the next-door garden. The lawn stretches in front of him like a desert. He leans back against the wooden slats of the fence, breathing hard. He closes his eyes. He should never—

"Boy!" He opens his eyes. Anna stands before him. Close up, he can see she is taller than before, but still the same Anna; her eyes are bluer and her dark hair longer. "Come!" And she runs straight down the length of the fence to the back of the house. Here there is another yard, another maid's room, and a door she pulls open. "Quick, in here!"

The door slams, she is gone, and he is left alone with the relief that floods through him. In the gloom he can just see a workbench, a few tools on it, a vise clamped to it, an old dog basket, and at the end of the room, behind a pile of broken furniture and under the workbench, a space. In he goes. His mouth is dry. He is so thirsty, he wishes he'd had more of the beer.

He closes his eyes, wraps his arms around his knees, and makes himself as small as he can, as small as he had been under the stairs.

"*Sssst.*" He can hear a hissing noise somewhere, and he drags himself out of a deep place where he is running and running after a person he knows to be Tsumalo, who is retreating and retreating before him across a desert he has to cross to get into Botswana. He has been trying to call out, but all that would come out of his mouth was a tiny dry croak, like a young frog's.

"Here, have this!" He opens his eyes with a start, and there is Anna, crouching beside him: yes, taller, up close, but still smaller than him. Less plump, bangs in her eyes, and holding out a mug of water. He drinks it down so fast, he almost chokes.

"What are you doing here?" He doesn't even know how to answer this and lifts both hands in a gesture that says, *I couldn't begin to explain.*

Instead he asks, "Are they gone?"

"Yes."

"Is it safe to come out?"

"No. Stay for a bit."

"Thank you." He waves the mug at her and smiles suddenly, a big, happy smile, and she smiles too.

"Where have you been?" she asks. "It's been two years. I was worried that you had been killed, like Tsumalo. The police released your mother, and she left for the Ciskei. Mrs. Malherbe's son took her away. But we never knew what happened to you."

"No," he says, and hesitates. Should he tell her? "I was in the camps. They are training soldiers to come back with bombs. To carry on the struggle." He stops. What can she know, this pampered little white girl? Yet she had helped him without a shadow of hesitation. There is something different about her now. A certain wiry strength, a watchfulness about the eyes; she is less strident, more considered.

"Thank you," he says to her again. "Now I must go."

Chapter Thirty-one

He is out in the road, running in the light dusk, keeping close to the hedges. In a minute he is back outside the Browns'. But there is something strange about the way the gates are standing ajar, one gate wider than the other. And where are the dogs? He turns on his heel just as he sees from the corner of his eye a flash of blue uniform. A policeman!

There is a yell, a guttural swear word he can't quite hear, and the air burning in his throat and his lungs. He didn't know he could run so fast. He rounds the corner onto Links Road and shinnies up and over the six-foot wooden fence and into the garden on the far side of Anna's house.

In the middle of the lawn there is a fishpond. Sitting on a bench by it is an elderly white man, alone in the half-dark beside a seated stone Buddha. He scrambles to his feet. Outside, in the road, they can both hear the heavy tread and the sonorous breathing of the policeman as he passes. "Boy!" he shouts. "Just you wait, *bliksem*, just you wait."

Joshua fixes his gaze on the old man and raises a shaking finger to his lips.

Their eyes stay locked until the heavy breathing and the footsteps have faded. Joshua places his hands together in the prayer position and bows his head. "Thank you," he mouths. The man inclines his head in response. And Joshua might be wrong, but he's sure he can see the glimmer of a smile.

He is with the Browns in their study.

They had heard the sirens and rushed down to the shed to warn him. And when he wasn't there, they'd panicked.

Fat Mrs. Ellis from across the road had blabbed that she had seen a black boy going into the Andersons' garden and it was known they were away. She was worried he might be a burglar. So the police had come. Poor Margie had had the devil of a job calming them down, says Mr. Brown.

Margie had said the boy was her grandson but that he was gone now, gone to catch the bus to Jo'burg; she had just been giving him some supper. Then the police had started a house-to-house search. They had burst into the Browns' garden; the dogs had escaped through the open gates.

The fish in their cases gape at him; they are frozen, as if they are still swimming, pewter bodies curved, mouths open. He wondered how it must have felt, deep and safe in the cool green ocean, and then the slice of the hook and the terrible fight, and the thrashing and drowning in the bright upper air.

Mr. Brown and Mrs. Brown are sitting side by side on the brown leather sofa, holding hands. He has never seen grown-ups holding hands. He can see they are frightened and he does not blame them. He is a liability.

"Joshua." It is Mr. Brown. He is frowning, and he squeezes his wife's hand as he speaks. "You can't stay here any longer. It was safer for you to lie low. But now the police have come"—and he gives an involuntary shudder—"you really need to go. They could come back and finish their search. And who knows what that might turn up."

Joshua knows instantly that there are things in this house that must not be found by the police. There may be hidden weapons or things that in other countries would not matter—like certain books.

"Of course I will go," he says quickly. "I will go now, if you like."

"No," says Mrs. Brown. "That would be dangerous for you."

She explains that Joshua is to leave the following morning. They will take him to the bus station. There he will not take a bus, but he will be picked up and taken to the Ciskei, back home, back to his mother and the twins, his grandparents; back to school.

He realizes that he doesn't want to go. He wants to stay in this city by the sea, with the mountain and the shanty-towns and the fierce dogs and the nasturtiums. And even the police and the Black Marias. He can feel the heat and familiarity of all these things with an intensity that surprises him.

But then he closes his eyes, and he can hear Tsumalo's

voice: "If you are going to be a free man, you must know how to read."

He can hear him say, "You are better than a son."

He can hear him say, "You and I will be free one day."

And he thinks, *Viva Ngenge. Tsumalo is King. I will never forget you.*

But there is one thing he still has to do. So after he has thanked the Browns and said good night to them, he takes the flashlight they gave him and pads back down the concrete path, shoes in hand, and climbs over the locked gate, laying his jacket over the spikes. He uses the loquat tree to get into Anna's garden; he finds her window and showers it with little pieces of gravel until she wakes.

This time, he is going to tell her where he is going.

Chapter Thirty-two

The next day is hot. Mrs. Brown gives him a pack of sandwiches, a foil packet of Romany Creams, and a thermos of tea, two sugars. He stows them in his rucksack, along with some of her son's old clothes. They all climb into the station wagon, and Joshua sits in the back like a laborer being given a lift to the bus stop. He slouches down in his seat, the tweed cap pulled low.

His head prickles with the heat.

As the car pulls out of the driveway, he looks up. The tarmac shimmers. He blinks: at the crossroads by the house stands Mrs. Malherbe. She is leaning down, her close-cropped, shingled hair gleaming in the sun, silver now, not pepper and salt. And she is holding the hand of the little boy from the shopping center. As he looks up at her, Joshua sees the clear blue eyes under the blond bangs. Of course; he is Robert's son.

A moment later they have crossed the road, turned left, and are out of sight: but that is when things begin to happen.

A Black Maria screeches to a halt across the road in front of the car. Mrs. Brown screams. Mr. Brown hits the horn hard. "Go!" he says without looking around, opens his door, and jumps out. "Officer?" he calls, polite but puzzled.

Joshua surprises himself by rolling out of the far-side door, springing to his feet, and running like a deer around the corner. He does not look back, though he can hear shouts. Above him are the close-leaved branches of the oak trees; he grabs the thickest branch he can see and swings himself up onto it.

Not a moment too soon. He sits, not breathing, as several pairs of feet pound beneath him along the road. He doesn't look down. If he does, he might fall. And if he falls, he might never stop falling. He puts a hand into the pocket of the jacket Mr. Brown gave him and into which he had put Sindiso's gun this morning. It is still there.

He knows that if the policemen come back along the road, he could kill one of them — but only one. And he remembers what Sindiso said when he asked for a gun of his own: "If you have a gun, you will be one person with a gun. And they will all have guns. So you will be killed."

So now he is a boy on his own with a gun. He wonders what has happened to the Browns. Have they been arrested? He wonders what will happen to the dogs. He thinks about their son in America. He thinks about all of these things as he sits in the tree on Links Road, just along from the tree in which Tsumalo had sat so long ago. All day he sits, his hands aching from holding on to the branches, until the sounds of the search begin to fade away, and dusk begins to fall.

He looks down through the leaves. He can hear there is

a car coming slowly along the road, and he stiffens, holding his breath, as it comes into view. It is a red Alfa, roof down. He can see a head of curly brown hair. The man pulls the car over and gets out. He begins to walk along under the trees, looking around him and calling softly for his dog.

"Betsy," he calls, "come here, girl. Betsy!"

It is Robert. Joshua and he both know that Betsy is not there.

He stops and listens. Then, very quietly, he says, "Joshua? Are you there? I've come to take you home."

Joshua closes his eyes tight. He can see his grandparents' house and the dusty road that leads to it. He can see himself running down it calling, "Mama! Mama!"— and there they are, all of them, crowding out of the little building, calling his name: his sister, his brother, his grandmother, his grandfather, and then, at last, his mother. There are tears streaming down her face like a waterfall.

"I'm coming," he whispers, and he begins to climb down.

Glossary

amandla—Xhosa for "power"; a rallying cry during the fight against apartheid.

bergie—Afrikaans for homeless person

Black Maria—police van with a steel cage on the back to transport prisoners

bliksem—Afrikaans for "lightning"; derogatory term, roughly translates as "bastard"

boetie—Afrikaans for little brother

Ciskei and **Transkei**—"homelands" or "Bantustans" that were part of the apartheid system, areas created like Native American reservations, supposedly to act as home territories for the black population. They covered a fraction of the area of "white" South Africa, although the black population was far larger. The people who were based there needed passes in order to work in the "white" part of the country.

doek—Afrikaans for head scarf

duiker—a small African antelope

hamba kahle—Xhosa for farewell

hayi—Xhosa for no

jislaaik—Afrikaans exclamation of astonishment

mielie-pap—maize porridge, a staple food in southern Africa

moegoe—Afrikaans slang for "twit"

mos—Afrikaans for "after all"

safe house—a house where freedom fighters could find shelter

stoep—Afrikaans for "veranda"

suurvygies—a ground-growing succulent (the name translates as "sour figs") whose fruit can be made into a preserve

tamatie-bredie—Xhosa for lamb stew with tomatoes

tjoek—Afrikaans slang for "prison"

tokolosh—Xhosa for the little evil spirit who haunts bedrooms

Umkhonto we Sizwe—"Spear of the Nation," the military wing of the African National Congress (ANC), which was the main revolutionary organization fighting the apartheid government, and which formed the first truly democratic government of South Africa

Author's Note

I grew up as a privileged white child surrounded by poverty and deprivation that we largely didn't see. This was a world in which it was illegal for a boy to live with his mother, in which black people not only did not have the vote but barely had a legitimate existence, in which those on both sides of the conflict were brutalized.

I wrote *The World Beneath* because this was the world that I grew up in, and it was why I left South Africa for England. The South Africa of 1980 — still reeling from the murder of political activist Steve Biko and from mass bannings of publications and people — was a dangerous place for a newly qualified journalist, and those who were brave enough to stay often ran into trouble with the police, like my fellow students whom I wrote about in *Class of '79*.

The house in *The World Beneath* was the house that I lived in; and although the boy himself does not exist and neither my family nor I feature directly in the book, we too had a black maidservant whose children were being raised far away in the Ciskei, and who, like many, was supporting them with no state help; I'm not sure if she had help from the children's father.

Our maid was also called Beauty. To my shame, I met only one of her children, just once, a bright and loving little girl whom I tried to teach to read. But she was just on a visit and soon returned to her grandparents.

I was outraged to learn that white children got their schoolbooks for free but that black children had to pay for theirs. Then, in 1976, my last year at school, the Soweto riots broke out, and it was shocking to hear of all the children who were shot.

For many children and teenagers, the apartheid era in South Africa is not even a memory. They were simply too young when the last white government was in power, and if they recall Nelson Mandela, it will be as a past president of South Africa, not as its most famous political prisoner.

This is why I wanted to write about that time and about the rise of the anti-apartheid movement in South Africa.

Acknowledgments

First, to my daughter and son, Imogen and Dominic Warman Roup, for being unfailingly loving and encouraging. They were just seven and nine years old when the manuscript was first read aloud to them, chapter by chapter, and were extremely discerning and strict editors. Julian Roup, for keeping calm and keeping me fed through all those after-work work hours. And the usual suspects: Gail Walker, Fiona Powrie, Barbara McCrea, Jeanne Samuels, Liz Wildi, Tracey Hawthorne, Susie Rotberg, and Heather Meyerratken—my sister, and my sisters under the skin: they know what I owe them. My nieces, Kate and Hannah Walker, who, like their mother, were early readers. Joe Bond, for his encouragement during the darkest times. My beloved parents, Lynne and George, without whom none of this would have been possible. Ros Barber: poet, scholar, author of *The Marlowe Papers,* and my creative writing tutor at the University of Sussex. My editor and friend, the poet and children's writer Mara Bergman, for her patience and her faith in my ability—even when that ability was quite invisible to me—as well as her extraordinary skill in turning this into a book for the most discerning audience of all.

Janice Warman
East Sussex
January 2015

Amnesty International

The Universal Declaration of Human Rights says *"we are all born free and equal,"* but this was not the case in apartheid South Africa. *The World Beneath* points to some of the terrible realities of an unequal society.

We are all born with human rights, no matter who we are or where we live, but we are not always allowed access to them. Human rights are about justice, truth, and freedom. They are part of what makes us human. They help us to live lives that are fair and truthful, free from abuse, fear, and want. But they are frequently under attack, and we need to uphold them.

Amnesty International is a movement of ordinary people from across the world standing up for humanity and human rights. We aim to protect individuals wherever justice, fairness, freedom, and truth are denied. If you want to find out more about human rights, how to take action, and how to join or start one of our youth groups, go to www.amnesty.org .uk/youth. And if you're a teacher, you can find many free resources, including "using fiction to teach about human rights," at:

www.amnesty.org.uk/education

Amnesty International UK
The Human Rights Action Centre
17–15 New Inn Yard
London EC2A 3EA
020 7033 1500
www.amnesty.org.uk
www.amnestyusa.org
www.amnesty.org.au